W9-BMH-863

"We just need to get through the wedding tomorrow...

"Then we can go back to living our normal lives. You won't have to see me and I won't have to see you."

Phoenix's words struck him. He didn't like the idea of never seeing her again. The past few days had awakened something in him.

Carter kept his eyes on hers. She held his gaze. Old feelings returned, stirring his emotions. Perhaps those feelings had never left and remained dormant in his soul. His heart quickened. Desire flooded him and he wondered what Phoenix would do if he kissed her. She still hadn't looked away. Was she waiting for him to leave? Did she want to kiss him as much as he wanted to kiss her? Maybe she was having some of the same wild thoughts. Maybe old feelings were coming to the surface for her, too.

Carter stepped closer to Phoenix. She didn't move. Carter noticed the rise and fall of her chest become more intense. He stepped closer. She stayed put. He watched her throat shift as she swallowed. He smelled the sweet scent of perfume. He wondered if he could taste the salt on her skin...

* * *

One More Second Chance by Nicki Night
is part of the Blackwells of New York series.

Selected praise for Nicki Night

"Nicki Night does an outstanding job creating characters with a dynamic chemistry that you could feel bouncing off the pages."

—*Book Referees*

"I loved the chemistry between Ethan and Zoe! I could not put this book down."

—Five-star *Goodreads* review on *Intimate Negotiations*

NICKI NIGHT

ONE MORE SECOND CHANCE

If you purchased this book without a cover you should be aware that this book is stolen property. It was reported as "unsold and destroyed" to the publisher, and neither the author nor the publisher has received any payment for this "stripped book."

Recycling programs for this product may not exist in your area.

ISBN-13: 978-1-335-73508-9

One More Second Chance

Copyright © 2021 by Renee Daniel Flagler

All rights reserved. No part of this book may be used or reproduced in any manner whatsoever without written permission except in the case of brief quotations embodied in critical articles and reviews.

This is a work of fiction. Names, characters, places and incidents are either the product of the author's imagination or are used fictitiously. Any resemblance to actual persons, living or dead, businesses, companies, events or locales is entirely coincidental.

This edition published by arrangement with Harlequin Books S.A.

For questions and comments about the quality of this book, please contact us at CustomerService@Harlequin.com.

Harlequin Enterprises ULC
22 Adelaide St. West, 40th Floor
Toronto, Ontario M5H 4E3, Canada
www.Harlequin.com

Printed in U.S.A.

A born and bred New Yorker, **Nicki Night** delights in creating hometown heroes and heroines with an edge. As an avid reader and champion of love, Nicki chose to pen romance novels because she believes that love should be highlighted in this world, and she delights in writing contemporary romances with unforgettable characters and just enough drama to make readers clutch a pearl here and there. Nicki has a penchant for adventure and is currently working on penning her next romantic escapade.

Books by Nicki Night

Harlequin Desire

Blackwells of New York

Intimate Negotiations
One More Second Chance

Harlequin Kimani Romance

Her Chance at Love
His Love Lesson
Riding into Love

Visit her Author Profile page at Harlequin.com, or nickinight.com, for more titles.

You can also find Nicki Night on Facebook, along with other Harlequin Desire authors, at Facebook.com/harlequindesireauthors!

One

"Don't become bridezilla, Savannah!" Phoenix Jones closed her eyes, took a deep, soothing breath. She massaged her temples with her fingertips. "It's all going to work out just fine, sis. Don't get worked up." Phoenix spoke in a calming tone. "In less than forty-eight hours we will be on a plane to one of the most beautiful places on this globe. Let that sink in." Her sister was like their mother, Nadine. Dramatic. Phoenix was more like their dad, not easily rattled.

"But she knew what day we were leaving. I told her several times." Savannah's voice was laced with frustration. Her pitch grew higher and higher. "What if it's not ready by tomorrow night?" Her voice cracked. "What am I supposed to do about a veil at this point? I'm going to end up getting married without one! It should have been done a week ago."

Phoenix realized her sister was on the verge of tears. "Honey," she said softly, "it will be ready. I'll call her myself and reiterate how important this is for you. And if it's not ready, we'll pick some of the most exotic flowers that Fiji has to offer and make a beautiful crown to place on that pretty little head of yours. You may be working yourself up for nothing. Let's wait and see what happens. Okay?"

"Ugh!" Savannah huffed. "There's still so much to do. I don't see how I'm going to get it all done."

"You're a perfectionist. No matter what happens, your wedding will still be perfect because that's just how you operate. It will be fine. I promise you. We've got a lot to do, so don't let this stress you out too much," Phoenix said.

"I'll try." Savannah sounded defeated.

"I'll come by after work to help with anything you need. Cool?"

"Thanks." Her tone was flat.

"Girl! You're about to get married to the man of your dreams on the island of your dreams at the wedding of your dreams. I'm going to need you to sound a little happier."

Phoenix could hear Savannah sigh through the phone. She wanted her sister to feel better. Planning a wedding wasn't easy. Even though Phoenix's wedding never happened, she knew firsthand how stressful they were to plan.

"You're right. I'll try to calm down. See you tonight?" Savannah asked.

"What time do you want me there?"

"Seven good?"

"See you at seven, sis. And try not to drive your husband-to-be crazy before I get there."

"I can't make any promises. Love ya!" Savannah let out a small laugh and Phoenix returned the sentiment.

After ending the call, Phoenix sat back and smiled for the first time since she arrived at work that morning.

Phoenix's day started with tension. Actually, the tension began the evening before when Brent, the guy whom she'd been seeing, started questioning her about a conversation she'd had with her male coworker and friend. He wanted to know why her coworker had called her after business hours. That was normal for their team. They were close and often spoke outside work. If they got great ideas, they'd call to run them by each other. Brent's jealous nature was coming to the surface along with a few other red flags, and Phoenix didn't like what she'd been witnessing. She ended their dinner by telling him it was best for them to go their separate ways.

Her cell phone rang and she picked it up. Phoenix's boss, Indra Lee, asked her to come join the team members in the conference room. Phoenix could tell by her boss's tone that she didn't have good news to share. Needing a few minutes to brace herself for whatever was about to come, Phoenix swung her office chair around to face the windowed wall. She never tired of the view down Sixth Avenue. The rhythm of New York City pulsed. She took in the picturesque landscape with neat rows of traffic-filled streets framed by magnificent tall buildings. Usually, this view soothed her mind, but at the moment the pressures of life dulled the joy she got from gazing at the skyline.

Grabbing her cell phone, pad and a pen, Phoenix headed to the conference room as instructed. The two women were the only females in Aida, a small, male-dominated technology firm that created technological platforms using AI—artificial intelligence—to help improve systems for small and midsize companies. As one of Aida's founding partners, Indra recruited Phoenix and helped her develop into a leading tech professional. In the few years that Phoenix had been with the company, they'd grown exponentially and shared their good fortune with their staff. Phoenix loved what she did and got paid extremely well for the work she put in. What more could she ask for?

As Phoenix made her way to the glass conference room in the center of their sleekly designed office, she hoped that whatever they had to meet about wouldn't add extra work to her plate. She was leaving for vacation in two days and already had too much to close out before her departure. When she entered the conference room, the look on Indra's face didn't give Phoenix hope. Indra's smile seemed forced, apologetic almost. Technology moved so fast that it made the industry volatile. Phoenix hoped she wasn't losing her job.

Phoenix sat and waited. Over the next several moments their team of twelve employees made their way into the conference room, engaging in small talk. It was obvious that the others weren't sure why they were there, either. Indra sat at one end of the conference table and her partner, Dean Ochoa, sat at the other end. The two sighed simultaneously before Dean nodded. Indra took that as her cue to begin speaking. The simple sound of her voice called everything to order. The staff members who were standing took seats. The room settled into a quiet hush. Indra started by thanking everyone for coming. Phoenix found that odd. The next words that came from her mouth shocked everyone in the room, except Dean.

"I know." Indra looked around at the surprised expressions in the room. She pressed her lips together after dropping a verbal bomb. Some team members looked stunned, others sad and a few faces were completely blank. "This is big news, though bittersweet."

Bitter. Yes. For Phoenix, there was nothing sweet about what Indra had just said. She didn't know how to feel. Had her boss just told them that their company had been sold and was moving clear across the country to Silicon Valley? What did that mean for Phoenix?

Dean began to speak as if he'd heard the question in Phoenix's mind. "This will be a big ask, but we want to offer all of you the opportunity to stay with the company." Dean paused.

Indra picked up where he'd left off. It was like a well-choreographed dance. "That would mean you'd have to agree to move to California with us. Unfortunately, they want all of our employees in California so there won't be any opportunities to work remotely from here."

"Yes." Dean jumped back in, shaking his head. "Much of this work is tech focused and can be done right from our computers, but our team has proven to work better and smarter when we're physically together. That's what makes us so strong."

"We're prepared to offer generous relocation packages," Indra added, taking back the verbal baton. She looked around and tilted her head sympathetically. "I know this is a bit of a shocker. But I promise you it's really, really good news. Jabber has made us an offer we would be foolish to refuse. This is a huge opportunity. We do understand how you might feel, but we would be delighted to keep our entire team intact."

Phoenix's head filled with questions but she found it difficult to speak. Jabber, a technology giant, had been gobbling up smaller tech firms for the past few years. However, they didn't just buy any company—only companies they knew would earn them billions. The fact that they considered buying Aida was a testament to how successful they'd become. Their offers were often too generous to leave on the negotiation table.

Phoenix didn't want to leave New York. Her entire family was here. She'd visited the Bay Area, but never entertained the thought of living there. What if she did move? She'd miss her family terribly. Her dad was scheduled for hip surgery after the wedding. Phoenix was sure she'd have to pitch in and help her parents out while he healed. If she stayed? She'd have to find a new job. She raised her hand. Questions continued to fill her head.

"Phoenix." Indra called her gently, like a teacher giving her young student the floor to speak.

Despite the softness, Phoenix felt somewhat betrayed. How could Indra have kept something this huge from her? "How much time do we have to make our decision?" Phoenix heard herself ask. It was like an out-of-body experience. She felt blindsided and hadn't shaken the feeling yet.

Indra seemed to have squirmed a bit. She possibly knew how Phoenix felt.

"Six weeks." Dean interjected.

A collective gasp blew through the room. Murmurs ensued.

Dean held a hand up, quieting the room. "In six weeks these offices will shut down and we will officially move into our new offices just outside the Bay Area. We'd greatly appreciate your decision within the next two weeks so that we will know what our hiring needs are. We'd also like for all of you to stay on for the full six weeks and will compensate your dedication."

The room went silent again as everyone digested what Dean had said. After a few moments Indra broke the silence. "For those of you who decide not to join us, we hate to see you go. You are family." She paused and inhaled slowly. Indra blinked rapidly as if she was fighting back tears. "We're prepared to give you a generous severance package. Our hope is that it will fill any salary gaps while you seek out other employment opportunities."

"Well, that's very nice of you, Indra and Dean," Delano, one of the software engineers, said. "I don't need six weeks. I can tell you right now that I will not be able to relocate. Our daughter is just a few months old and my in-laws are caring for her while my wife and I work. In fact, my wife just started a new job. My siblings and I take turns caring for our aging parents. I hate to pass this up but the timing is just not right for me."

Indra pressed her lips together and tilted her head. Delano was sitting next to her. She placed a supportive hand on his shoulder. "We understand."

"We'd love for you to stay on for the full six weeks. It's okay if you need time here and there for interviews. Are you willing to do that?"

Delano shrugged. "I'm happy to."

"Thank you," Dean said.

A few others explained why they would or wouldn't be able to make the move. Some were excited and started side chats about apartment shopping and Bay Area hot spots. Phoenix remained quiet, taking it all in. There was too much to consider to make a decision like this so quickly. She didn't have children but she did have a pretty robust life and a close-knit family. Recently, her father started having a few health issues. Phoenix and her sister had been helping their mother with their dad's doctors' appointments. Perhaps with fewer family issues and more time to prepare, she could have been more excited about moving across the country. She hadn't thought about leaving New York and wasn't sure she wanted to.

After a few more questions from the staff, the meeting was called to a close. Phoenix went to her office, shut the door and quietly sat facing Sixth Avenue. Then she lifted her head and stared at the ceiling. She got lost in thoughts around the offer that Indra and Dean had made. A light tap at her door caught her attention. Indra pushed the door open slightly and stuck her head through the small opening.

"Can I come in?" Indra asked.

Phoenix looked at her with a sideways glance and twisted lips. After a sharp exhale she said, "Come on in."

Normally, she wouldn't speak to her boss that way, but Indra had become her friend. She flashed Phoenix an apologetic look.

"How come you didn't tell me?" Phoenix chided.

"I'm sorry, Phoenix," Indra said. "Legally, I couldn't utter a word to anyone. I didn't even tell Rich," she said, referring to her husband. "He found out when the ink dried on the deal the other day."

"You know you can trust me." Phoenix was hurt.

"Of course, but any missteps could have blown the entire deal," Indra said. "I hated to drop this bomb on you just before your vacation but we wanted to make the announcement when everyone was in the office, and today was our first chance to do it. Besides, they didn't give us much time to make the transition. They want us in their headquarters ASAP. I had to push to get the six weeks."

"Silicon Valley?" Phoenix rolled her eyes. "That place is overrun by twelve-year-old gamer geeks."

Indra laughed. "You're so silly." She sat on the corner of Phoenix's desk. Her smile faded and her face turned serious. "You coming?"

Phoenix grunted and let her head roll back. "That's a big decision."

"I know. But what's holding you here? Try it and if you don't like it, come back home."

"It's not that easy," Phoenix said.

"I don't want to lose you. To be honest, moving is the only part of the deal I tried to fight. Rich won't be joining me until the end of the school year. I'm going ahead to get things settled. He and Cody will come in a few months. We didn't want to disrupt Cody's school year. I guess I'll fly back and forth as much as possible until my family gets there."

"Are you excited, Indra?" Her question came across more solemn than she intended.

Indra put her hand on her heart. "Extremely. This is the deal of a lifetime."

Phoenix held her hands in the air. "That's what matters most. Congratulations."

Indra slid off the desk, walked around to Phoenix and put a hand on her shoulder. "Why don't you take tomorrow off? Start your vacation early and give yourself time to absorb all of this. Think about joining us in California and let me know what you decide."

"Thanks, but I have too much work to do before my vacation. I promise I'll give this serious consideration."

"That's all I ask," Indra said.

Phoenix watched Indra leave her office. She knew that whether she went or stayed behind that she and Indra would likely stay in touch, yet she couldn't help but feel like she just lost one of her closest friends.

"What else could happen?" Phoenix asked aloud and regretted the moment the words left her lips.

Two

Carter Blackwell wished he could snap his fingers and magically appear at the airport. This vacation couldn't have come at a better time. The volatile stock market had made a few of his high-net-worth clients extremely anxious. He'd been trying to alleviate their anxiety on calls day and night. A major business opportunity recently gained steam and he needed to make some major decisions to move forward soon. And he was in his cousin Jaxon's wedding. Carter, Jaxon, his brothers Lincoln and Ethan and a few friends had recently returned from a long weekend of partying in Las Vegas. That was more than a week ago and Carter still hadn't caught up on his rest. Now he had to deal with the pressure of closing a number of loose ends before leaving for vacation in less than two days.

With work, his business venture, family and a robust social life all operating at a high, Carter was weary and desperately needed to unplug. He was more than ready for the beauty and serenity of Fiji.

Carter looked at his watch and took a deep breath. The afternoon seemed to have passed without his realizing it. In another thirty-six hours he would be on the airplane, leaving all of these worries behind him for ten days. That made him smile.

Carter had meant to leave work a bit early to get a jump on packing. He hadn't even pulled his suitcase out yet. He contemplated turning off his work cell phone but decided against it. There were still a few major stops he had to make before heading home.

The moment his foot hit the stoop of his brownstone near downtown Brooklyn, his cell phone rang.

"Hey," Carter said through a smile as he greeted the woman he'd been dating for the past few months. This was one call he didn't mind taking. Her company, among other things, could help ease his mind.

"Um," Sinai Killington sighed. "We need to talk."

Carter's smile faded. *What now?* "Something wrong?" he asked.

"Have you made it home yet?" Sinai asked, not directly answering his question.

"Just getting here," he said as he turned the key and pushed the door open. "You're still coming tonight, right?"

Carter heard her clear her throat. "Yes. I'll be there in about twenty minutes."

"Okay." Silence ensued. After a few beats Carter asked. "Everything all right?"

"We will talk when I get there."

"Okay," he repeated. "See you soon."

Sinai ended the call without saying goodbye. Carter looked at the display wondering what happened.

Brushing off the abrupt end to their call, Carter placed his keys onto the hook in the kitchen. Standing still, he took a deep breath, and then rubbed his tight shoulders and sore neck. He worked out regularly, but this wasn't soreness from the gym. Carter understood this tightness to be the tension that had been building from a long, grueling workweek. He hoped that whatever Sinai wanted to talk about wasn't going to be too heavy. He already had so much on him.

Sinai's visits usually helped him relax. She was sleeping over the next two nights so they could get up and catch their early flight to Fiji. They weren't exclusive but they really enjoyed each other's company. Carter felt like if he really wanted to get serious in a relationship, Sinai would definitely be a top contender. She was smart, beautiful, ambitious and great in bed. She didn't take life too seriously and was always ready for a good time.

All of Carter's friends were getting married. Out of his brothers, he was the only one who wasn't in a committed relationship. Even Ethan had snagged a beautiful wife and now they had a baby on the way.

He looked around his home. It was perfectly suitable for a family, but Carter wanted to raise his children on Long Island where he'd grown up. He'd always imagined a large home buzzing with warmth and activity even though he wasn't ready for all of that now. Not yet.

More than not being ready, Carter didn't believe he had come across the *right* woman yet. He'd dated his share of beautiful women, but he was looking for much more than beauty. Sinai had a lot going for her, but... What exactly was he looking for? Carter wasn't sure. Phoenix was the one whom he'd let go. Was he looking for another version of her? Carter shook his head as if to get rid of that thought. That bridge had burned and was pretty much unsalvageable.

The doorbell rang, bringing Carter out of his thoughts. He realized he hadn't made it beyond the kitchen since he arrived at home. He thought about all the packing he needed to do as he headed to the door to let Sinai in.

"Hey," Carter said after he opened the door. He leaned forward to kiss her pink glossed lips.

"Hey." Her response was flat. She puckered but didn't kiss him the way she usually did.

Carter stepped aside to let her in. He admired her pretty face and curvaceous figure as she walked into his brownstone. His brow furrowed when he noticed she wasn't carrying a suitcase.

"You need me to grab your bags from the car?" he asked.

Sinai stopped walking and slowly turned around. "I'm not going, Carter."

Carter reared his head back. "What? Why?"

Sinai dropped her hands to her sides. "Carter…" She paused, trying to find the right words. "It's time for us to go our separate ways."

Carter closed the door pensively. "What's this about?"

Sinai chuckled. "I know you've been super busy lately, but you couldn't have been so busy that you didn't see this coming." She stepped closer to him, rose on her toes and kissed him.

Carter kissed her back but was still confused. He stepped back and studied her brown eyes. "I don't understand."

"It's been a few months now and we have not progressed as a couple at all. I feel like I'm just a friend and you have no intentions on making me a true girlfriend. The other night made that painfully clear."

The other night? Carter wasn't sure what she was referring to. He scrunched his face. "The other night?" he asked aloud.

"Dinner the other night..." Sinai tilted her head. "You don't remember," she said matter-of-factly and shook her head.

Carter tried to think of what had happened.

"While we were at the table, my friend London asked about what's next for us. Your response was, 'We're just having fun.' It's been almost six months, Carter." Sinai's hand flopped against her thigh. "I want more than to just have a little fun. You've invited me to join you in Fiji but I've never met a single family member of yours. It feels awkward to meet them for the first time at your cousin's wedding and you have no desire to commit to me in any way. I don't want to experience Fiji like this."

Carter opened his mouth to say something.

Before he could speak, she smiled softly and held up her hand. "Let me finish, please. This isn't easy for me." Sinai paused a moment before speaking again. "You avoid any conversation that touches on a future when it comes to us. I've ignored these signs for a while but now I understand you don't want more. You're content. This..." Sinai waved her hand as if presenting the space around them. "This is fine with you." Sinai paused again. "But it's not okay with me." She placed a hand across her heart. "I want more, Carter. I deserve more."

Carter opened his mouth. Realizing he had no rebuttal, he closed it.

"It's okay, Carter. Really."

She was right. She was like a friend with benefits all this time. He liked her but didn't see being with her for the long haul. His inviting her to Fiji was about having more fun. It wasn't about taking anything to the next level.

"No hard feelings, Carter. I'm a big girl. I get it and I'm okay. At least now I am. At one point I hoped things would change but I have to do what makes me happy."

"I'm sorry." Carter quietly acknowledged the reality they were standing in.

"I'm sorry, too. It would have been nice." Sinai touched his face. "Going with you to Fiji wouldn't make sense for me if nothing is going to change. I hope you understand."

Carter looked at the ceiling and then back at her. "Is there someone else?"

Sinai tilted her head and grinned. "No. There's no one else."

"Oh," Carter said. He wasn't sure what else to say. This was unexpected.

"I really enjoyed our time together," Sinai said.

"Me, too." Carter touched her face. He stared at her for a moment. "So this is really goodbye?" Carter tried to absorb what was happening.

Sinai took the hand that Carter gently placed on her face and planted a soft kiss in his palm. "Yes." She closed her eyes and sighed. "This is goodbye." She smiled again. She blinked and a lone tear rolled down her cheek.

Carter's chest tightened. He felt bad but he didn't want to mislead her. He wiped her tear with his thumb. "You deserve the best."

"Thank you. I agree." She giggled. More tears fell. "You're a good dude, Carter. Maybe one day you'll come to believe in love."

Carter let her words bounce off him. There was too much happening in his head for him to think clearly. The one thing he knew was that it was time to let Sinai go. It was only fair.

"Goodbye, Sinai."

Sinai puckered her lips. Carter lowered himself to meet her. Their kiss was brief and sealed the fate of their relationship.

Sinai grinned, patted his chest and said, "Enjoy Fiji." With that she left, leaving Carter to absorb the moment and her absence.

Carter watched Sinai leave. He stood unmoving, stunned by what had just transpired. Sinai's words played over and over in his mind. *Maybe one day you'll come to believe in love.* She was the third woman in the past year who'd mentioned his apparent lack of belief in love. Admittedly, he was more interested in his career. That came first. He looked around his beautiful home. Suddenly, it felt empty. Carter brushed off the coolness that had settled over him.

There was too much to do. He had to pack. He faced major business decisions. Work was demanding. A relationship would just have to wait.

Three

The entire bridal party traveled together except Ethan and Zoe Blackwell. Zoe was expecting a baby and wasn't feeling well before the flight so they opted to change their departure so she could see her doctor before leaving.

As a gift to the bridal party, Savannah and Jaxon invited them to arrive a few days early to party and bond prior to the wedding. It was a token of their appreciation for agreeing to travel halfway across the globe on just a few months of notice.

Phoenix strolled through the hotel lobby and out the back to the area where the villas stretched out over the water. The grounds were lush and vibrant, with beautiful tropical plants lining the walkways. The colors were more vivid than the images the resort boasted on their website. She entered her villa and reveled in the breathtaking views of the ocean right outside her room.

The flight from New York to Fiji was more than fifteen hours. Then their group boarded a seaplane for another forty-five-minute flight to the private island where they would stay for the next ten days. Phoenix helped Savannah with last-minute preparations the night before leaving so she hardly slept. She was especially happy to see that her sister's veil had arrived in time. When Phoenix got back to her house, she packed and repacked several times to make sure she had everything she needed. Despite how exhausted she was, she didn't sleep well during the flights. Maybe it was the excitement of everything that kept her from getting rest.

Phoenix's body hit the plush mattress in her villa like a large piece of lead. She needed a nap if she was going to be able to get through the welcome party later that evening. She looked forward to all the festivities despite feeling a bit uncomfortable about having to be around her ex-fiancé, Carter. She was over him, but it still felt awkward knowing they would be in such close proximity for so many days. She managed a small smile and had actually said hello to him when she saw him at the airport. That was the extent of their communication. Their families lived in the same neighborhood and socialized in the same circles since they were children, but since the breakup, they had managed to keep their distance from one another.

Phoenix felt like she was sinking into a cloud of plushness on the king-size bed. She looked at her cell phone. The welcome party would start in a few hours. She rolled over onto her back and studied the leaf-like blades whirring on the ceiling fan, aware of how heavy her eyelids were becoming. Thoughts of how much fun and relaxation she was looking forward to having in Fiji carried her to sleep.

Banging on the door woke Phoenix with a start. At

first, she thought the knocking was in her head. She didn't realize she'd fallen asleep until this moment. She stretched and then sprung from the bed. "Coming!" she yelled through her yawn. Savannah was calling her name.

"Geesh!" Phoenix said when she opened the door. She walked back through the spacious villa toward the balcony with Savannah in tow. "What's going on?"

"You weren't answering. I knocked hard because I figured you had fallen asleep. We have a little issue," Savannah said.

Phoenix whirled around. "What happened?" She was ready to protect her younger sister.

Savannah stopped in her tracks and flinched at how fast Phoenix spun around. "Let's go sit on the balcony and I'll explain everything."

Phoenix narrowed her eyes at Savannah. "Okay," she sang. "You're making me nervous."

Savannah huffed but said nothing more until they reached the balcony. The ladies sat. A slight breeze greeted them. Savannah closed her eyes and lifted her face to the sun. She remained like that for a few moments. Phoenix followed suit.

Savannah exhaled and started to speak. "It doesn't look like Ethan and Zoe are going to make it."

"Oh no! Is she okay?"

"The doctor sent her to the hospital. She'll be there a few days under observation. When she goes home, she'll be on strict bed rest."

"Oh!" Phoenix's hand spread across her chest. "Poor thing. I hope she's going to be okay. She seemed so excited about this baby when I met her at the engagement party."

"Yeah. Ethan said she's pretty scared, but he's by her

side and his mom is staying back so his dad will be coming by himself."

"Wow. This is so unfortunate. How's Jax taking the news?"

"He'll be okay. He hates that Ethan and Zoe will miss everything but he just wants her and the baby to be okay. It would be heartbreaking if they lost that baby."

"Of course. How about you? Are you okay?" Phoenix asked Savannah.

"I'm fine. Just hoping for the best for them. I'm going to try to speak to her again tomorrow."

Several moments passed in silence.

"Phoenix."

The way Savannah said her name made Phoenix raise a brow. "Yes, Savannah?"

Savannah grunted but said nothing.

"Spit it out!" Phoenix admonished.

Savannah closed her eyes and the words rushed from her mouth. "Jax wants Carter to replace Ethan as his best man."

Phoenix's entire body stiffened. She tried her best not to show any emotion. This was her sister's wedding and she refused to do or say anything to ruin it. But something about having to walk down the aisle arm in arm with the man who had walked away from her the night before their wedding didn't sit well.

"Phoenix?"

She couldn't say the words running through her mind so she kept her mouth clamped shut.

"Fifi?" Savannah softly called her by her nickname. This time she leaned forward and looked into Phoenix's face.

"Yes, Savannah?"

"Say something. Please."

"I told you when you announced your engagement to Jax not to worry about me. This is your wedding. You and Jax have to be happy. I will be fine. I meant it then and I mean it now."

Savannah threw her arms around Phoenix's neck. "Oh! Thank you, Fifi! I was so worried. I love you, sis! I didn't want you to feel uncomfortable. Jax went over to talk to Carter. We wanted to make sure you two were okay with everything." Savannah's words spilled from her lips so fast she had to catch her breath when she finished.

Phoenix returned her sister's tight hug.

"Thank you for understanding." Savannah continued. "I may not be a big fan of Carter, but he and Ethan are not just Jax's cousins, they're the best of friends." She sighed. "I was so worried. I'll let Jax know. I told him you were over Carter anyway." Savannah stood. "Let me get back. The welcome reception is about to start and I still have to get dressed. See you there, okay?"

Savannah rambled when she was nervous. Phoenix stood with her sister and placed a hand on her shoulder. "Don't be nervous. Everything will be fine. See you at the reception."

Savannah took a deep breath. "Okay." She went to leave and paused. Turning back toward Phoenix, she asked, "Are you sure you're okay?"

"I'm fine." Phoenix placed her hand or Savannah's back gently.

"Say the word, sis, and I'll tell Jaxon it won't work out."

Phoenix waved away Savannah's concern. "It's all good. I get it."

Savannah hugged her sister tightly. Then, she left. Phoenix closed the door and leaned her back against it.

She didn't know how to feel but she couldn't let on that she was not happy about this new arrangement. Walking down the aisle with Carter at anybody's wedding would require strength that Phoenix wasn't sure she could manage.

What else could go wrong? Phoenix slapped her hand across her mouth. She thought it but refused to say it. Every time she uttered those words the universe found a way to show her.

Four

Carter paced back and forth in his overwater bungalow. He couldn't believe his fate. Carter knew he'd have to be around his ex-fiancée, Phoenix, and he'd prepared for that. The two hadn't spoken much at all since that fateful night before their wedding. It wasn't for lack of trying on his part. Once he told her that he couldn't marry her she didn't want to hear anything else he had to say. In fact, he never got the chance to explain why he needed to call off the wedding. That was five years ago.

Despite living in close proximity and occasionally seeing each other at functions, it was years before Phoenix would even acknowledge his presence. Eventually, she'd utter a contrite greeting here or there but it was nothing he could count on. He'd wanted to explain the whole story to her on several occasions but it was too late for that now. The pain had been buried. He'd been hurt, too.

Calling the wedding off was the hardest decision of his life but he was left with no choice.

He stopped pacing long enough to look at his cousin Jaxon, who was sitting on the sofa in the living room of the bungalow. Carter shook his head at Jaxon. “Does Phoenix know?”

Jaxon inhaled, held his breath a moment and then exhaled with a grunt. “Savannah is telling her now.”

“I don’t want to make anyone uncomfortable.” Carter shook his head adamantly.

Jaxon stood up from his chair and shrugged. “Neither do I, but without Ethan there’s no one else I’d pick for my best man besides you.”

“Yeah.” Carter parked his hands on his hips and groaned.

“Who wouldn’t expect that?” Jax said.

“Ugh!” Carter laid his hand across his forehead. “You know she hates me, right?” he asked, referring to Phoenix.

Jaxon waved him off. “She doesn’t hate you, man.”

Carter stopped pacing and looked at Jaxon sideways.

“Okay, maybe she does hate you just a little but that was a long time ago.”

“Not long enough,” Carter said.

“Five years, dude! You both moved on since then—dated other people. You just have to walk down the aisle with her after the ceremony. What is that? For two quick minutes you’ll have to be close to one another. You can survive that, right?”

“And what about all of this other stuff you and Savannah planned for this week? This…this team building…stuff. Clearly, we have to spend a lot more time around each other than a walk down the aisle after the ceremony.”

Jaxon sank into his shoulders. “Savannah just wanted

everyone to bond before the wedding. We wanted you all to have a good time."

Carter just stared at him.

Jaxon walked closer to him. "Come on, man. Tell me this isn't going to be fun. Four-wheeling? Zip-lining? Kayaking? Yacht parties?"

Carter lived for these activities. "Of course they'll be fun," he admitted.

"All kidding aside, Carter, you have to be my best man. Without Ethan, it has to be you. I need you, man," Jax repeated.

Carter threw his hand up. "You know I'll do anything for you. It's just that this…this is…ugh! This won't be fun. You and Savannah will have to somehow be the buffer. I don't know how Phoenix is going to respond to this."

"Look. Phoenix is a smart, reasonable woman. I'm sure she'll understand."

Carter wasn't so sure. Yes, Phoenix was intelligent. Brilliant, even. But she was also scorned by Carter. She'd proven time and time again that she wanted nothing to do with him.

"Think about this." Jaxon interrupted Carter's thoughts. "Maybe, if you two dare to become cordial enough, you could finally have the chance to tell her why you called off the wedding in the first place."

Carter stopped pacing abruptly and huffed. "That would probably ruin this entire trip."

"Think about the fact that you could finally be able to close that chapter."

Carter glanced at Jaxon and looked away, waving him off. "That chapter has been closed."

"Yes. You're over it. I get that, but you know what I mean. After all this time she still doesn't know. You,

Uncle Bill, Aunt Lydia, Ethan, Lincoln and I are the only ones who know the whole story. I never uttered a word to Savannah. She just thought you were a jerk with cold feet that wasn't ready to give up your bachelor ways. Maybe if you told Phoenix, she wouldn't hate you so much."

Carter plopped on the couch and let his arms fall heavily to his sides. "Do you have any idea how many times I tried to talk to her? She never wanted to hear it. She can't see any reason for me to call off the wedding on such short notice. She wouldn't even give me the chance to explain that night."

"I get it. She was hurt. She…" Jaxon searched for the right words.

"Felt rejected." Carter filled in the blank for him.

"And embarrassed," Jaxon added.

"I know." Carter felt bad all over again.

"Look. All I'm saying is that if things don't go crazy, maybe you guys can be cordial enough to perhaps have a normal conversation. This may be your opportunity to let her know the truth even if it happens after the wedding is over. She deserves to know."

"Maybe." Carter wouldn't cosign Jaxon's idea just yet. He knew it would take work to get Phoenix to hear him out, and ten days in Fiji might not cut it. Why bother at this point anyway? Weren't both of them over it?

"It's hard enough to deal with the fact Ethan is going to miss my wedding and I pray that Zoe is okay. We never imagined moments like this without each other. The most important thing is making sure their baby comes out healthy and strong. You with me?" Jaxon held out his hand.

Carter stood, took Jaxon's hand and pulled him in for a hug. "I'm with you, Jax. Let's hope this goes over well with Phoenix."

"Let's hope. Either way, we will get through this together," Jaxon said. He threw his hands out to the sides. "Dude! We're in Fiji! I'm about to get married!"

A huge smile spread across Carter's face. "Sounds like it's time to celebrate!" Carter walked over to the bar inside his villa. "Let the celebration begin." He poured two glasses of scotch and handed one to Jaxon.

They held their glasses up and clinked them together. Carter began to say something.

"Uh uh uh! Save it for the toast. Until then, let's just have fun."

The two men lifted their glasses again and threw the amber liquid down their throats.

"Ah! Nice," Carter said.

"Yeah," Jaxon said, putting down his glass. "We need to get ready for the welcome reception. Let me get back to my villa before my wife-to-be sends out a search party."

Jaxon headed for the door and paused. He turned back toward Carter and chuckled. "Maybe this is fate."

"What are you talking about, Jax?"

"Sinai decided not to come. Ethan can't come. And now you and Phoenix will walk down the aisle together. There might be something to this."

"Man!" Carter picked up one of the pillows on the sofa and tossed it at Jaxon.

He ducked, avoiding the hit, and hurried toward the door. "Just a thought." Jaxon chuckled. "See you at the reception." He let himself out and Carter could hear him laughing beyond the closed door.

Carter couldn't get mad. If the shoe was on the other foot, he would have teased Jaxon just the same. That was how they were with each other. Carter poured himself another drink and sat on his balcony overlooking the pristine water surrounding his villa. This time he sipped the whiskey slowly, wondering what these next few days could bring.

Carter hadn't had a serious relationship since Phoenix. Although he thought he was doing the right thing back then, he'd hurt Phoenix badly. But what could he do about that now? That was the past. He had his whole life ahead of him and several other large fish to fry. He just needed to get through the rest of the festivities and this vacation. He needed to enjoy himself. He deserved this break.

Big decisions awaited his return to the States. Carter looked forward to his time in Fiji being somewhat of a reprieve before starting new chapters in his life. Chapters that he was excited about, despite making other people unhappy, namely his father. While he was away, perhaps he could find the right words to let his father know that his days at Blackwell Wealth Management were numbered. Bill's dream for his sons taking over the company was dissipating. Carter had other plans and he'd sacrificed enough of his time to appease his dad. It was time for him to strike out on his own. Losing that promotion to Ethan was a turning point for Carter. Bill had given each of them the chance to prove themselves when they opened their branches. Ethan's branches out-performed Carter's and Dillon's giving Ethan the upper hand. Now his brother was his boss. It was time to make *his* dreams come true, not his father's.

Carter walked back inside and put his glass in the small sink on the wet bar. He didn't have time to ponder the past. He had an entire future ahead of him despite the challenges it held. Right now he was in Fiji on a well-deserved vacation, ready to have fun and celebrate his cousin and his beautiful fiancée. Carter wasn't about to sit around mulling over what could have been. He did what he had to do. As for what was next, when he got back home he would do what was necessary. Right now it was time to party!

Five

Phoenix dressed for the welcome reception that was taking place under a cabana on the beach. Her strapless, flowing maxi dress was perfect for the seaside festivities. Phoenix closed the tube of nude lip gloss and stared at her reflection in the bathroom mirror. She took a deep breath, sighed and rolled her eyes toward the ceiling. "It's for Savannah," she said to herself.

Savannah's wedding was the important thing here, not her own feelings about Carter. How bad could it be? A walk that wouldn't last more than a few minutes couldn't be so terrible.

Phoenix groaned. She wished it could have been anyone else. She and Carter were supposed to walk down the aisle together as husband and wife five years ago. That never happened because he called it off the night before the wedding. She never anticipated fate would bring her to a moment like this. She was over the situation and wasn't interested in ever getting close and personal with Carter ever again. This trip would be the first time in years that they would have to spend time around each other in close proximity for more than a few minutes.

"This is for Savannah," she repeated as she stuffed her gloss, mascara and eyeliner back into her makeup bag. "I'm going to have a good time."

Phoenix put the bag inside her suitcase, straightened her back and headed out her villa door. As she made her way through the tropical surroundings and smiling natives, she decided not to let the circumstances bother her. She moved on from Carter a long time ago. One stroll down the aisle for her sister's wedding wouldn't change a thing.

Other than tight cordial greetings at events by mutual friends, she and Carter never talked. All she had to do was to continue being cordial. Carter was just another ex.

By the time Phoenix reached the area on the beach where the reception was being held, she was smiling. It could have been the ocean breeze caressing her skin, the beautiful scenery or the fact that she was finally starting to settle into her vacation. Regardless of what it was, Phoenix was happy to feel free of all worries. The next ten days were going to be amazing, fun and peaceful. That was just what she needed.

A handsome Fijian gentleman handed her a colorful drink as she approached the cabana designated for the reception. She smiled and waved at Lincoln and Ivy, Carter's siblings, and continued through the space. The bridal party was small and made up of mostly family. It was originally eight members but now that Zoe and Ethan had to stay behind, there were six of them left that included Carter, Lincoln and Jaxon's buddy Angel. Carter's sister, Ivy, was among the women along with her and Maya, Savannah's good friend. Angel and Maya were the only members of the bridal party that weren't family.

Because a few changes were made, and Carter was now the best man, he was partnered with Phoenix in the wedding since she was the maid of honor. Lincoln was walking with Maya, and Angel was paired with Ivy.

Phoenix hugged and kissed Maya when she stepped under the cabana. Maya and Savannah were college roommates and had become inseparable in the past few years. You would have thought they were friends since childhood. She greeted the others, chatting briefly as she sipped her drink and enjoyed the ocean breeze. Carter and Lincoln hadn't arrived. She continued mingling.

Phoenix would be around everyone for most of the trip and didn't mind, but she also longed for a few quiet moments. She spotted a cozy-looking chair near a corner of the cabana and excused herself from the small crowd. That would give her some quiet time until her sister and Jaxon arrived. They weren't the quiet types.

Phoenix thought about their engagement as she sat. It certainly wasn't a long one. They'd known each other since grade school and weren't interested in a long engagement. The day after Jaxon proposed they scheduled a date a few months out and began planning for their destination wedding. Savannah dreamed about marrying in exotic locations since she was a teenager.

Phoenix ran her hand across the white leather covering the comfortable chair and wondered how they managed to keep them so clean. Phoenix looked around and took in the all-white decor, curtains, seating and flowers, and smiled. The space looked pure, fresh and blissful.

Phoenix took a sip of her drink, closed her eyes and lifted her chin. She could smell the sea and taste the salt on her lips. She felt like all of her worries could roll away with the waves. She listened to the melodic Fijian music playing in the background. With her eyes still closed, she swayed to the rhythm.

"I see that you're enjoying the vibe."

At the sound of that voice, Phoenix felt a bit of her peace slip away. She opened her eyes to find Carter standing over her. Her heart quickened. Not because she was annoyed by him disturbing her moment, but because Carter looked unreasonably handsome. More handsome than the last time she saw him. She figured it was the beauty of Fiji filtering everything around her.

"Hello, Carter," Phoenix said and nodded before sitting up straighter. Taking a sip, she looked at him over the rim of her drink. "It's nice to see you." That was all she had to say. Phoenix hadn't thought about actually having a conversation with him.

"May I?" Carter gestured toward the chair adjacent to her.

"Sure." Phoenix sat back, getting comfortable again.

For several moments they sat in silence. Phoenix wondered how long Carter would stay seated next to her. She closed her eyes again and tried to get back into the music. Her heart rate had returned to normal and the initial tension she felt from Carter's presence was waning. Perhaps this wouldn't be as grueling as she'd anticipated.

After a while Carter finally spoke. "It's beautiful here."

"Yes. It is." Phoenix hadn't opened her eyes.

After another long pause Carter began again. Phoenix gave him her attention. "I just wanted to say hello and..." Carter paused. That made Phoenix open her eyes. Carter blinked in that thoughtful way that Phoenix remembered him doing whenever he was choosing his words carefully. "Having to walk down the aisle with me is probably the last thing you want to do. I just wanted to let you know that I understand if it makes you uncomfortable. I'm doing my cousin a favor and other than that, I'll stay out of your way."

"Same." Phoenix flashed a quick, cordial smile. "You don't need to do this, Carter. I'm sure you had the same conversation with Jaxon that I had with my sister. It's about them, not us."

"I'm glad we're on the same page," Carter said.

"Me, too," Phoenix agreed.

Silence expanded between them again and so did a sense of awkwardness. She thought about asking for another drink. Hers was getting low. Maybe Carter would say something else. They were no longer used to sharing companionable silence. Instead, Phoenix felt the strain of his presence. She thought about coming up with small talk but she sat in the thickness of the silence instead.

"By the way, you look amazing," Carter said.

Phoenix didn't know why his compliment made her smile. But what ex didn't want to hear that they still had it?

"Thanks."

"Hey, everybody!" Savannah burst onto the scene, holding Jaxon's hand. Relieved by her arrival, Phoenix took note of how happy her sister looked and how lovingly Jaxon looked at her. "Are you all ready to get this party started?" Savannah's cheerful voice carried throughout the cabana. She and Jaxon took the drinks the Fijian gentleman handed to them.

"Yeah!" Several members of the wedding party raised their glasses and shouted.

Savannah and Jaxon's arrival succeeded in breaking through the tension surrounding Carter and her.

"Let's start with a toast to beautiful Fiji." Savannah raised her glass. "And I want to toast to each of you for accepting our invitation to come a few days early."

"Yes," Jaxon interjected. "We're a long way from home and Savannah and I wanted to take this time with you to show you our appreciation. So the next few days will be filled with a bit of fun and adventure on us."

"So we can thank you." Savannah picked up where Jaxon left off. "Thank you for agreeing to be a part of our special day, for being here and for being amazing family and friends."

"Cheers!" Jaxon said.

Everyone who had glasses raised them and repeated, "Cheers."

After a sip, Savannah continued. "As you know, Ethan and Zoe won't be able to join us this week. We spoke to them and Zoe is stable but won't be able to leave the hospital for several days. We wish them well."

A few people groaned. Ethan's and Zoe's presence would definitely be missed.

"Since they couldn't join us, I want to thank my cousin Carter for stepping up and taking on the role of my best man." Jaxon raised his glass toward Carter. "Love you, man."

Phoenix noticed Ivy look from Carter to her, and then lock eyes with Lincoln. This was news to them too.

"Love you back, dude! Anything for my little cousin."

"We all know you're older, Carter!" Jaxon teased. "We'll be sure to remind you of that when it counts the most." A few chuckles erupted from the crowd.

"We've put together a schedule so you'll know what to expect."

Savannah and Jaxon talked for a few more moments to let everyone know what they'd planned over the next few days. Phoenix was well aware of the plan since she worked with them to schedule some of the excursions. She looked forward to having a good time but suddenly wondered about the activities that required partners. For some of the excursions, she and Savannah had paired the members of the wedding party based on who they were walking with. This meant that she would be paired with Carter. They would definitely be too close for comfort. She was fine with being around Carter as long as they kept a cordial distance. Phoenix quickly realized that walking down the aisle with Carter wasn't the only time she'd have to engage with him.

Lost in her thoughts, Phoenix missed the last few moments of Savannah and Jaxon's announcement. "Now, let's party!" Phoenix heard Jaxon yell.

Phoenix looked to the side and noticed Carter watching her. Savannah nodded at the woman assigned to assist her with the wedding party. The lady disappeared for a moment and then reggae music blared from speakers settled in the sand. The party officially started. Everyone danced with drinks in their hands, surrounding the soon-to-be newlyweds, cheering and shouting their names. All seemed to be lost in the excitement of the moment except Phoenix.

Phoenix looked at the happy couple in the center of the bridal party as they danced. Jaxon and Savannah's love for one another oozed into the atmosphere. Unbridled joy danced in their eyes as they gazed at each other and moved to the reggae beat. Phoenix attempted another discreet glance at Carter but he was no longer watching her. Yet, like her, he didn't seem caught up in the fun like the others. Or perhaps, like her, he needed something else to look at besides the blissful couple. Watching them love so open and intimately made Phoenix realize how far she was from that in her life.

Six

Carter pulled out his phone and sent a quick text to Ethan to check on Zoe's status. He acted instinctively, not thinking about the time difference at first. The day was new in Fiji, but with the seventeen-hour time difference it was almost midnight back in New York. Ethan was a night owl. Carter was pretty sure he was still awake. And he was. Ethan texted him back almost immediately, letting him know there was basically no change in Zoe's status. She was still in the hospital but in good spirits and he was right by her side. Their mom had left the hospital a few hours before.

Carter knocked on the door to Lincoln's villa, which was right next door to his, and turned his face toward the rising sun as he waited for him to come out.

"Ready to go," Lincoln said as he stepped outside.

"You look tired," Carter said.

"I was up late so I could talk to Brit and the kids.

They can't wait to get here. I see you and Phoenix are playing nice so far."

"Yeah. No reason not to."

"I know, but I imagine it must still be a little awkward."

"It is," Carter admitted.

"Wait!" Lincoln stopped walking. "What happened to Sinai? I just noticed that she wasn't here. I thought she was coming with you."

Carter released a sigh that ended in a chuckle. "Yeah. We're not dating anymore."

Lincoln reared his head back. "Since when?"

"The night before I left. She said I wasn't ready for a commitment, and coming here with me wouldn't have helped our situation."

"Ha!" Lincoln snickered.

"What's so funny?" Carter asked but already knew the answer. No one knew him better than his brothers. Before Lincoln could answer, Carter had already started laughing with him.

"Didn't the last one say that?"

"Is it that obvious?"

"Don't worry. When the right one comes along you won't have to question that."

Jaxon walked into the hotel lobby where he met up with Carter and Lincoln. "What's up? You guys ready?" Jaxon rubbed his hands together as if he was plotting.

"We're ready," Carter said and looked at Lincoln for confirmation.

"Let's do this," Jaxon said and looked around. "I see the women haven't made it here yet, but our chariot awaits." He pointed to the shuttle bus idling in front of the hotel. "I'll let the driver know we need a few more minutes."

Just as Jaxon stepped out of the hotel doors, Carter noticed Phoenix and Savannah making their way toward them. Phoenix was gorgeous. She always had been a flawless beauty—at least to him. He tried not to be obvious but couldn't turn away until he'd taken all of her in. Her hair was pulled back into a ponytail, revealing every beautiful detail of her face. Carter remembered the way he used to trace the outline of her dimples and place his finger in their deep crevices. It always made Phoenix smile harder. He remembered being the one who kept a smile on her face. The simple denim halter and shorts with gold sandals that Phoenix wore gave her a youthful appeal. Carter tore his gaze away, assured that she had not noticed him watching. He remembered so much about her in that moment. There were plenty of other beautiful women out there, possibly less stubborn than Phoenix.

"Good morning!" Carter gave the ladies a cheerful greeting.

"Good morning," Phoenix said in return and nodded at both Carter and Lincoln.

"Hey, guys!" Savannah said. "Where's Jax?"

"He just went out to talk to the shuttle driver."

"Thanks! See you outside." Savannah headed toward the exit.

Carter looked beyond Phoenix and saw his sister, Ivy, walking with Maya. It looked like most of them were there. He was sure that Angel wasn't far behind. He waved at the approaching ladies and headed out to let Jaxon know.

The crew boarded the bus. Carter expected to get some sleep during their hour-long ride but Jaxon and Savannah had other plans. They played trivia, asking questions to see how much their family and friends knew about their relationship. As tired as Carter was, he enjoyed himself.

"Okay, next question," Phoenix said, giggling.

"This isn't fair!" Maya said, folding her arms and pouting playfully. "You guys have known them all your life. You have all the answers."

"She's right," Jaxon said. "Let Angel and Maya try to get this one before any of you chime in," he instructed.

"That's not fair," Carter said.

"You just want all the damn prizes," Carter's sister, Ivy, said.

"What? I'm competitive." Carter shrugged.

Laughter filled the shuttle.

"Here's the question. Where did Jaxon and I meet?"

Maya jumped up. "I know this one. Grade school, right?"

"Yep. Which one."

"Pr..." Carter started.

"Unh uh uh!" Savannah put her finger up, stopping Carter from answering. "You can't answer! We all went to the same school, silly. Of course you know. Give Maya a chance. Geesh. I should have picked more creative questions." Savannah laughed.

"Wasn't it something, something prep school?"

"Close enough!" Jaxon laughed. "You get a point for that one."

"See, Carter, I know some of this stuff." Maya gave Carter a look that appeared more flirtatious than friendly.

Carter thought he noticed a vibe coming from her at the reception the night before, but brushed it off. He figured she had to know that he dated her best friend's sister. *Dated* was putting it lightly. Weren't there some girl codes that she was possibly violating? He glanced over at Phoenix. She didn't seem to pay attention. That was fine, too, since there was absolutely nothing going on between the two of them, and based on their history, the chances of anything ever happening between Phoenix and him were extremely slim. Maya was a beautiful woman, but dating her was out of the question. It was too close to home.

That thought made Carter wonder about the possibility of becoming more than cordial with Phoenix, and immediately shook that thought away.

They moved on to another game. This once pit the men against the women. Soon after, they arrived at the destination.

"Okay, guys! We're here. Oh my goodness. This is going to be so much fun. I really hope you all enjoy this. I know you will, Carter. You and Phoenix love adventure."

Carter looked at Phoenix. She gave a quick smile and turned her head.

The tour guide boarded the shuttle and gave everyone instructions. The woman spoke perfect English despite her Fijian accent. The more she spoke, the more Carter became excited. This was his kind of excursion, one that would take away all the tension he'd been holding in his body for the past several weeks. He was ready to let go and live.

The group grabbed their knapsacks and got off the bus. They browsed a gift shop on their way to the area where they were to be matched up with horses. The beautiful animals were their rides up the mountain.

Carter chose a stunning jet-black stallion and wasn't surprised when he saw that Phoenix chose a gray-and-white one that looked like the one she rode back home as a teen. She'd named him Sparkle because of its flecks of gray coloring. It took nearly a half hour to get to their destination. The well-trained horses followed one another in a straight line with the tour guide in front and another employee for the tour company trailing the group from behind. Carter assumed that they wanted to ensure there were no stragglers.

Carter actually closed his eyes a time or two during their ride up the mountain. He breathed deeply, taking in the clean, fresh air. He looked out over the mountain terrain, which seemed like lush, natural artwork. Carter watched the leaves move with the breeze. He had all but forgotten about every worry he'd left behind. By the time they reached the area where they were to dismount the horses, he'd also forgotten about keeping his distance from Phoenix. Carter was caught up in a blissful peace.

"That was nice."

Carter looked up, a bit surprised that Phoenix had actually said something directly to him. He hesitated a moment to make sure before responding. "Yes. It was."

"I needed that," she said.

"Me, too."

"How are you guys doing?" the tour guide said.

"Great. Wonderful. Fantastic." These were some of the responses.

"Some of those paths were a bit narrow, don't you think?" Maya said. "I'm glad that ride is finally over. Wait! How are we getting back down the mountain? Do we have to get on those horses again? I'd rather walk." Maya shook her head.

Savannah laughed. "Come on, girl." She took Maya by the hand. Worry about that part when we get there."

"Savannah!" Maya groaned. "That was scary. My horse walked way too close to the edge of the cliff. I closed my eyes and started praying. I mean, I know God hasn't heard from me in a while, but I promised if he got me through that trail, I'd reach out to him a whole lot more."

Savannah held her stomach and doubled over laughing. The rest of them laughed, too.

"Maya! You're nuts," Savannah said. "Come on, more adventure awaits!"

Maya moaned and followed Savannah.

Carter chuckled the whole time. Maya was beautiful, but her personality was over-the-top. Even if he hadn't dated Phoenix in the past, he would have to pass on dating her. She wasn't his type.

"On the way back down, maybe I could ride on the back of Carter's horse. He seemed to have a good handle on his stallion."

Carter raised a brow. Maya's comment was bold and her tone seductive. He wasn't expecting that. From the look on everyone's faces, neither were they. Maya flashed a flirtatious smile. Ivy, Lincoln, Jaxon and Angel all looked at Carter at the same time. Ivy barked out a laugh. Lincoln raised a brow. Angel snickered. Jaxon shook his head. Phoenix gave no reaction at all.

"Girl, come on." Savannah yanked Maya's arm. "You'll be fine."

"We have a short hike to our next activity," the tour guide chimed in, bringing everyone's attention back to the excursion.

Moments later they arrived at a platform and were fitted for gear to zip-line. The guide explained that there would be sixteen zip lines and the highest point was 16,400 feet in the air.

"Sixteen thousand! Oh, Lord! Where's my horse?" Maya shouted. "I can't do that."

"Yes, you can," Savannah said.

"You can go alone or partner up if that makes you

feel more comfortable," the guide said in an attempt to calm Maya.

"Carter, will you partner with me?"

"I'll go with you," Savannah said quickly before Carter could respond.

Carter was caught off guard again. As a ladies' man, he always had a quick comeback for a pretty woman. Maya was coming for him hard and fast. But this was different. He didn't feel comfortable flirting like that in front of Phoenix.

"Don't you want to go with Jaxon?" Maya asked Savannah.

"We always go by ourselves," Jaxon interjected.

"If it makes you feel safer, I'll go with you." Carter felt obligated to say something. Savannah and Jaxon were trying their best to clean things up.

"That's okay, Carter. I'll go with her. She'll scream your ears off," Savannah said.

"Okay." Carter shrugged.

Glancing toward Phoenix, Carter wondered again if Maya knew anything about their history. Phoenix still seemed unfazed. Maya and Savannah's friendship blossomed after their breakup so there was a chance that she wasn't aware of Phoenix's and his relationship.

"Okay, guys. Here we go," the guide said in a melodic accent.

Lincoln clapped his hands together. One of his frequent gestures. "I'm ready for an adventure."

"Yeah!" Jaxon pumped his fist in the air.

"Ha!" Carter chimed in with a laugh.

The crew hooked Maya and Savannah up first and sent them soaring across the zip line. Maya screamed the entire way, leaving the rest of them on the platform chuckling.

"Saved by Savannah, huh?" Lincoln said, looking at Carter.

"She's coming for you hard, brother," Ivy said and then looked at Phoenix. "She must not know."

"It's not a problem, Ivy." Phoenix waved away any concern she appeared to express. "Maya wasn't around back then and the past is the past."

Carter chuckled and shook his head but something about Phoenix's cavalier attitude made him feel a certain way. What way? He wasn't quite sure but he felt something.

For the next hour they zip-lined at jaw-dropping speeds over treetops. From their vantage point, they took in breathtaking landscapes and views of the ocean. Then they explored caves with exotic ecosystems like nothing Carter had ever seen.

The last part of the tour included a therapeutic dip in the mud pool. Savannah grabbed a gob of mud and tossed it onto Jaxon's chest. Jaxon picked her up and sat down in the mud, covering Savannah up to her neck. Pure joy spilled from her lips as she laughed.

"What are you laughing at?" Savannah said to Phoenix after standing back up. She grabbed another handful of mud and tossed it at Phoenix.

Phoenix let out a sound akin to a hoot and slung some mud right back at Savannah. Savannah ducked and the mud hit Carter square in his face.

"Oh my goodness! I'm so sorry." Phoenix's hand flew to her mouth. Ivy howled, pointing at Carter.

"Who are *you* laughing at?" Carter slung mud in Ivy's direction and also hit Lincoln.

Before long, mud was being slung everywhere. Everyone was covered. They eventually exited the pool and lay in the sun to let the mud dry before a refreshing cleansing in the hot springs. After an authentic Fijian meal they headed back to the shuttle completely spent.

Maya switched her seat. This time she sat next to Carter. He had no trouble sleeping on the way back. At one point he woke to find Maya resting her head on his shoulder, and Phoenix looking his way. They locked eyes for a quick moment before she snickered, shook her head and turned away.

The sun was preparing to set when they were approaching the resort. Carter watched it for a while before nudging Maya awake. He looked around and noticed how quiet the shuttle bus was. They all had fallen asleep. He lifted Maya's head from his arm. He smiled out of kindness. He knew he would have to find a polite way to let her know he wasn't interested. The situation with Sinai was still fresh and something about flirting with Phoenix around didn't settle right.

Maya moaned and stretched. "You're going back to your room?" she asked Carter.

As forthright as Maya was being, Carter wondered if he'd heard her correctly.

"Pardon me?" Carter looked directly at her to make sure he heard her this time.

Maya twisted a finger in her hair and tilted her head. "Are you—" she touched his chest with her index finger "—going back to your room right now? Would you like company?"

Carter smiled. "Thanks, but I don't think that would be a good idea."

"Why? You scared?" Maya pouted.

"Not at all. But thanks. I'm definitely flattered."

Maya twisted her lips. "Well, you know where my villa is in case you change your mind."

Carter simply lifted his brows and smiled. He hung

back while everyone exited the bus. He specifically waited for Maya to leave.

"See you guys later," Ivy said. "I need a shower." One of the first to leave, Ivy waved at the rest of the crew and disappeared through the lobby.

"Lincoln, give me a second," he said to his brother, who was waiting to walk back to his villa with him.

"Phoenix…" Carter jogged to catch up with her.

Phoenix turned toward Carter. A slight smile played on the edges of her lips.

"Listen. I…there's nothing going on with Maya and me."

"Why are you telling me this, Carter?"

"I just felt you needed to know."

"There's also nothing going on between you and me. What you do with other women is none of my business."

"There's no need to get snippy, Phoenix."

"I'm not snippy!" she huffed. "You don't owe me any explanation. That's all I'm saying."

"I didn't say I did. I'm just trying to make this less… uncomfortable."

"Fine!"

Carter blew out a frustrated breath. "Maybe you could try being a little nicer."

"Nicer, Carter? Really? All I have to do is get through the next few days. This is about my sister and Jax, remember? Not you!" Phoenix's raised voice caught the attention of Lincoln, who was standing several feet away, and a few other guests.

Carter looked around and lowered his voice. "I didn't say it was about me. I was only trying to be up front."

"Thanks." Phoenix's voice was close to a whisper as she looked around. "It's not necessary."

"You know what…fine. Forget I said anything." Carter turned in frustration.

Carter walked toward Lincoln. "Let's go." His frustration wouldn't let him engage in any small talk as they walked back toward their villas.

Seven

The next morning, Phoenix almost missed the soft knock on her door. She looked out before letting Savannah in. Her sister was in a white swimsuit and matching cover-up. In fact, almost every outfit that Savannah wore was white. Between the white attire and the tiara brandishing the word *Bride* in sparkling crystals, there would be no mistaking who was the bride among them.

Phoenix plopped on the couch with one leg folded under her, sipping a cup of instant coffee. Savannah came and sat beside her.

"You okay, Fifi?"

Phoenix stopped midsip and looked at Savannah. "Sure. Of course. Why?"

"Maya's behavior yesterday, especially last night."

Phoenix rolled her eyes. "Why is everyone so worried about Carter and me? She could have him if she wants."

Savannah twisted her lips unbelievingly. "First of all, who is everyone?"

Phoenix tilted her head. "Why are you looking at me like that?" She closed her eyes for a few seconds before answering Savannah's question. "You and Carter seem to be so worried about how I feel about Maya. It's no big deal."

"You can talk that crap with anyone else but me. I know."

"That was in—"

Savannah held up her hand. "Yes. It was in the past. I know. But whether you still hold a torch for him or not, no one wants to see their ex frolicking with another woman so close to the fold."

"I do not—"

"Yes! Again. I know you no longer have feelings for Carter," Savannah said mockingly and then tossed Phoenix a sideways glance, but then her expression softened.

"What?" Phoenix groaned and then shrugged.

"I'm sorry." Savannah touched her sister's leg. "I knew you wouldn't love having to partner with him for the ceremony and we couldn't avoid having him here because he's so close to Jaxon, but I didn't realize how much this would affect you."

"What's that supposed to mean? I'm fine." Phoenix put her coffee cup down on the end table.

"Tell that to someone who will believe it. This is me, Fifi. No one knows you better. You haven't been yourself since we've been here. You've been trying so hard to seem unaffected by his presence that you're not even having real fun. I can see that you're just going through the motions. It makes me feel horrible."

Phoenix stood and walked toward the view of the water. "Trust me. I'm fine."

Savannah walked up behind her. "I saw the way you looked when Maya was coming on to Carter yesterday."

"Savannah!" Phoenix spun around and faced her sister. She didn't mean to call her sister's name so harshly, but Savannah was hitting close to home and she wanted this conversation to end.

Phoenix had to admit to herself that she still felt the sting of his betrayal, and even after five years she still didn't have a solid answer as to why he walked away from her the night before their wedding. She didn't want to care about it, but she couldn't seem to help herself.

"Savannah," Phoenix called her name gentler this time. "Please don't worry about me. This trip is all about you. Yes. It's awkward for me, but I'll get over it. I haven't been around him like this since before our break up. It just takes some getting used to. I don't care if Maya wants Carter. Who am I to stand in the way of that?"

Savannah stood firmly in her spot and folded her arms across her chest. "There's more to this. I know there is."

Phoenix looked away. "You're going to be late. We have another day full of adventure that starts in less than an hour."

Savannah dropped her arms. "We're not done with this conversation." She started toward the door. "I told Maya that you guys dated in the past but that was all I said."

That made Phoenix laugh. She walked behind her sister to let her out.

Savannah stopped in the frame of the door and turned back toward Phoenix. "Try to have some real fun today, please."

"I've been having a great time."

Savannah cut her eyes to the ceiling. She went to her sister and hugged her. "Don't be late," she called out as she left.

Phoenix closed the door and rested against the back of it. She thought she'd done a better job of hiding her angst. She had to let go. Whether she got the answers she felt like she needed or not, nothing would change. She and Carter were done. The pit of her stomach knotted. She wanted to be done, but truthfully, there were too many loose ends dangling for that to actually be possible. When everything had happened, she was in too much pain to hear what he had to say. What could he possibly tell her that would make things better? He turned her entire world around the night before the biggest day of her life. She kept everything in after that and tried to convince everyone she was fine. Maybe being around him now was bringing old anger to the surface. She wasn't interested in having Carter back, but maybe she was ready for answers. However, getting answers from Carter would require that she gave a few of her own and she definitely wasn't ready for that. What good would it do now? She decided to leave it alone.

Phoenix got dressed so she could meet everyone downstairs. Admittedly, she felt a little silly about her behavior the night before. It was actually considerate of Carter to reassure her about his intentions with Maya. The truth was Maya's flirtation *did* bother her. She just wasn't willing to admit that to anyone but she certainly felt that twinge of jealousy. She caught Carter's glances but refused to acknowledge them, wanting to appear unfazed. Despite her feelings, she vowed to have more fun for the rest of the trip. Why should she miss out?

When Phoenix reached the lobby, she tapped Carter's shoulder and asked if she could talk with him for a moment.

"What's up, Phoenix?" She could hear Carter's frustration with her in his response.

He had certainly put more effort into making this easier to deal with. She hadn't matched that effort until now. She promised to try.

"I wanted to apologize for last night. I shouldn't have snapped at you like that. Truce?" She held out her hand.

Carter looked at her outstretched hand for a moment before shaking it. "Truce. I'll continue to stay out of your way."

"No need. As two reasonable adults, I think we could manage despite the little bit of history between us. I'm sure you want to enjoy this trip as much as I do."

"Yeah." Carter chuckled. "A little bit of history."

"Just a little." She pinched two fingers together, jokingly. She saw Maya coming their way. "I know who'd like to make a little bit of history with you," Phoenix said, teasing him about Maya's flirting and then discreetly nodded in her direction.

Maya was cheerfully saying hello to everyone so Carter didn't have to turn around to know who Phoenix was referencing. "No, thank you!"

"Ha! Not your type, huh?" Phoenix said sarcastically but couldn't hold in her laughter too long. She of all people knew Carter's type. Both of them chuckled.

Phoenix felt lighter.

"Our next excursion awaits!" Jaxon yelled, capturing their attention. He waved one arm and grabbed Savannah by the hand to lead her to the shuttle.

"Hey, Phoenix." Maya hung back as the rest of the party headed outside. "Can I chat with you one moment, please?"

"Uh. Sure." Phoenix stopped walking and waited for Maya to catch up.

"Savannah said you and Carter used to date?"

"Yeah. Something like that," Phoenix said.

"All this time and I never knew that. I guess it's because I never really see you around when I'm with Savannah."

"I suppose," Phoenix said.

"That was before Savannah and I became really close, right?" Maya smiled. "He's really good-looking."

"Mmm-hmm." Phoenix nodded in agreement.

"Knowing that you two have history, I was just wondering how you felt about…you know…me flirting with him. I'm really harmless."

A barrage of words flashed through Phoenix's mind. "It's no big deal," and "as long as he's on the market," were the only ones she allowed to pass her lips.

Maya seemed to glow after Phoenix's comment. "Is he? I don't see that he's here with anyone."

Phoenix looked toward the ceiling and thought a moment. "Actually, I don't know."

"Okay. Thanks!" Maya practically skipped away.

Phoenix inhaled slowly and held it for a moment. She was having to work harder to stifle that twinge of jealousy the kept rising up.

Everyone boarded the shuttle, and two hours later they were riding quads across a dirt trail.

"Partner up! It's time for our relay race," Savannah said.

"Girls against boys!" Phoenix yelled.

"What? No! It wouldn't be fair. The girls would lose," Maya said.

"What girls!" Ivy and Phoenix said at the same time. They looked at each other, giggled and slapped high five.

"Me. This girl." She pointed at herself with both thumbs. "Didn't you see me lagging behind everyone?"

"Don't worry. The first round will be men versus women," Savannah said.

"We'll do a relay from here to that big rock over there," Jaxon said. "And then we'll pair up with our or original partners."

"And your partner is the person you're walking in with for the ceremony. So Phoenix, you're with Carter. Lincoln, you're with Maya, and Angel, you're with Ivy. And me..." Savannah looked at Jaxon and wiggled her shoulders. "I'm with my sweetie." She snuggled up against Jaxon.

"I wanted to be on Carter's team," Maya said but must have felt Savannah's eyes on her. "I'm sorry," she said immediately.

Phoenix and Carter looked at each other and shared knowing smiles.

Jaxon jumped on his quad next to Savannah's. "Babe. Should we apologize to them now for leaving them in the dust?"

Savannah threw her head back, laughed and then high-fived Jaxon. "Maybe we should."

"Don't waste your time. We got this. Right, Carter?" Phoenix said.

"No question," Carter answered confidently.

Phoenix and Carter weren't new to four-wheeling. It was one of their favorite things to do when they were together.

Maya caused the girls to lose the men-versus-women round. Unlike the other ladies, Maya wasn't very good at adventures like this. She complained at how dirty her sneakers were getting and how she'd have to toss them when they got back to the resort. They switched to partners. Each round became more competitive with Savannah and Jaxon winning the first, Angel and Ivy winning the second, and Phoenix and Carter winning the last two, which gave them bragging rights. Lincoln and Maya came in last each time. Maya's whining gave them much to laugh about.

Phoenix forgot how much fun Carter could be to hang out with. Together they talked trash about their double win. She looked over at Carter laughing and suddenly noticed how his ripped abs and athletic build pressed against his tank top. Being covered in splattered dirt gave him a sexy, rugged appeal. Something warmed her belly and she turned away, chiding herself for being turned on by Carter's confident stance, muscular arms and taut chest. She never could deny his good looks. And his laugh. Sound spilled from his lips like a baritone melody. She swallowed hard.

"Should we do one more time?"

"No!" Lincoln and Maya yelled.

"Yes!" everyone else said.

Savannah giggled. "Majority rules."

"We're ready to win again. Right, Carter?" Phoenix held her hands up in victory.

"Yes we are," Carter said.

"We were just getting warmed up," Ivy said and Lincoln cosigned with a nod.

Maya said nothing. Phoenix was pretty sure she knew she was the reason they'd lost.

The last race was the closest of them all. Savannah and Phoenix were neck and neck. One would gain a small lead and that would soon be devoured by the other. As they neared the finish line, Phoenix maneuvered around Savannah to get the win. Her ATV hit the side of a rock, causing it to flip on its side, tossing her from the quad. She flew through the air and landed with a thud, hurting her knee. She yelled in pain.

"Phoenix!" Savannah screamed, jumped off her quad and ran to her sister.

Everyone else got off their ATVs and raced to Phoenix rolling on the ground, hugging her knee. She groaned. Carter was the first person at her side.

"Phoenix! What hurts besides your knee? Where does it hurt?" Carter leaned over her.

"M…my…my knee." It took all of the breath in Phoenix's body to speak through the pain. Other parts hurt but her knee was by far the most painful.

"On my goodness, Phoenix," Savannah cried.

Phoenix looked up at all of them around her. Their eyes were filled with worry. Taking turns, they kept asking how she felt or if anything else hurt. Her aching knee took her breath away. She couldn't speak. Carter scooped her off the ground and carried her like a baby.

"We need to get her some help." Despite the weight of Phoenix, Carter moved swiftly. He positioned her on his ATV and jumped on. "Hold on tight."

Phoenix wrapped her arms around Carter's waist and leaned into his back, groaning from the pain. The rest of them jumped back on their quads and followed Carter as he cautiously maneuvered back toward the rental reception area.

"Just hold on." Carter was breathless, too. Phoenix could hear the concern in his voice. "I got you."

Phoenix moaned. It was the only response she could muster. Tears rolled down her face, wetting Carter's T-shirt. She nestled her face in the center of his back and allowed herself to cry.

"It's going to be okay," he assured her all the way back.

From the second that Carter lifted Phoenix into his arms, she knew innately that Carter would take care of her. The past didn't matter right now. Neither did Maya. What she felt in that moment almost shocked her as much as her accident did. Phoenix felt safe in Carter's arms. Like an old, familiar place, she felt like she belonged there.

Eight

Carter and the others paced outside the room as the doctor on-site examined Phoenix's knee. No one spoke. Fortunately, they didn't have to leave the facility for her to be seen. Carter thought they'd have to find a hospital but having someone on staff made sense. Surely, there were accidents all the time.

Savannah was with her. Carter wanted to be inside, as well. His heart felt like it dropped into his stomach when he saw her fly off the ATV. He couldn't get to her side fast enough. The way she hit the ground scared him. Hearing her yelp gave him a small bit of relief. Nothing mattered more in that moment than making sure she was okay.

Now, as they waited, he pondered his response. He didn't think; he reacted instinctually. Phoenix was in danger and he hurried to her side to help. Surely, if it had been his sister, Ivy, who had gotten hurt, or even Maya, he would have responded the same way. Of course he would have helped; yet, Carter couldn't deny that there was something about seeing Phoenix hurt that compelled him to be the first by her side. Maybe it was guilt.

Savannah came out of the room. Everyone looked toward her at the same time. Carter was next to her instantly.

"What did they say? Did she break anything? She's going to be all right?" The questions rushed from his mouth.

Jaxon put his arm around Savannah.

"She's going to be okay. It was a bad fall, but nothing is broken. She's got some swelling, bruising and pain of course. She's going to have to stay off her feet. They were giving her crutches but she refused them. The doctor insisted so she said she'd take one."

"That's Phoenix for you," Carter said. As pretty and dainty as she appeared to be, Phoenix was tough.

There was a collective sigh. "I'm glad she doesn't have any broken bones," Ivy said.

"He's giving her something for the pain now and said the shuttle could stop by the pharmacy on the way back so she can get some regular pain medicine. He didn't believe she needed anything that required a prescription. He's wrapping her up now and then we can go."

"Do you think she'll be up for game night later?" Maya asked.

"I don't know. The pills he gave her can make her drowsy. She may need the rest." Savannah laid her head on Jaxon's chest. "I can't believe this."

Jaxon wrapped his arm around Savannah and rubbed her back. Carter watched as he comforted her. The love they had for each other was undeniable. He wondered if he was even capable of sharing love like that with someone. Then his thoughts careened toward the unpleasant. This accident could have been much worse. Life was fragile and could be cut short at any moment.

The door opened and Phoenix wobbled out with a crutch on one side and the doctor supporting her on the other. Carter ran to the doctor's side and helped Phoenix along.

"Why all the somber faces?" Phoenix said, snickering. "Y'all are not getting rid of me that easily."

Relief was evident in everyone's sighs and expressions. Leave it up to Phoenix to act like this was no big deal.

"You scared the daylights out of me!" Savannah admonished, carefully hugging her sister. "Good try but you're still going to be in this wedding." She wagged her finger at Phoenix, pretending to be annoyed.

"Ah, man!" Phoenix steadied herself on the crutch and snapped her fingers. "Seriously. What's it going to take to get out of this thing?"

"It's a good thing your dress is long and will cover up that swollen knee. I don't want to hear anything about you not wanting to take pictures because your knee looks fat." The women laughed hysterically at Savannah's joke. She shook her head as if she was really frustrated. "Wait until I tell Mom how you tried to get out of my wedding."

The sisters' bantering put everyone else at ease. Moments later they had all climbed into the shuttle and were headed back to the resort. Phoenix sat in a row by herself with her injured leg across the seat next to her. Carter sat nearby to keep an eye on her. Before long she was fast asleep. Both the four-wheeling and the emotional toll had drained them all. One by one, they each fell asleep except Carter. He was wound up in his feelings and couldn't rest. Instead, he examined life as it was.

Carter thought about everything that awaited him at home, including the big decisions. Again, he thought about Sinai and her comment about him.

Then it hit him. Carter knew what his problem was when it came to a serious relationship. He couldn't control it. As an alpha male born with leadership in his DNA, Carter didn't like things he wasn't able to control. Maybe that was behind his need to leave the family business. His entire career has been under his father's thumb. And once he gave his heart to a woman, he was no longer in control of that, either.

Nine

Phoenix rested her head against a cushion and sank lower into the large spa tub. She added a few drops of the essential oils she'd traveled with. Lavender and eucalyptus was her favorite combination and just what she needed after the day she'd had. Phoenix had returned to her room both dirty and battered. Her entire body ached from her accident. Something else had been shaken that day. Her will.

Phoenix thought back to how Carter had run to her side, how he carried her and how she cried into his back. She remembered how safe she felt in his arms. It felt right. She didn't like feeling so at home in Carter's arms.

Phoenix had planned to let go and have fun but she didn't count on enjoying Carter's company so much. It had been a long time since she'd been this adventurous. She and Carter used to do those kinds of things all the time. None of the other men she'd dated since then thirsted for adrenaline rushes the way she and Carter had. They always had fun together.

Phoenix grunted. She wanted to stop thinking about Carter but he wouldn't leave her mind. She didn't want to be mad at him forever. Yet, she also wasn't looking to be his friend. There was too much pain between them for a friendship to work.

Phoenix took her time rubbing the scented scrub into her skin. Her knee throbbed, but not as bad as it did before she took painkillers. Again, Carter popped up in her thoughts. It was awkward being friendly with him. It wasn't like friendship was foreign to them. They grew up in the same community and considered themselves to be good friends even while they dated. But that changed when he came to her the night before their wedding and told her he couldn't marry her. What kind of friend did that? She was so distraught she wouldn't hear anything he said after those horrific words. No explanation seemed sensible. She screamed at him. Told him to get out of her house. She never wanted to see him again. He said he wanted her to keep the engagement ring. She took it off and threw it at him.

That following day was supposed to be the happiest day of her life. They had plans to share that joy with over three hundred guests at one of the Hamptons' most beautiful venues. Excited, her mother, Nadine, arranged for press, which Phoenix tried to talk her out of. The cancellation became the big story. The humiliation was publicized. She relived the pain of being jilted every time she had to explain to someone new that the wedding was off. Phoenix's parents were furious, especially her mother, and the relationship between the families was strained for the next few years. She distanced herself from Ivy, also. Though they knew each other growing up, they'd grown much closer as Phoenix was planning her wedding. Once it was called off, she distanced herself from Carter's siblings, as well. Phoenix sucked her teeth, bringing herself back to the present.

She got into the tub to relax, not to get assaulted by her past.

"Dammit, Carter!"

She was supposed to stay mad at him. It was better when she kept her distance. Feelings of anger were easier to manage than what she was feeling now. Phoenix couldn't articulate what she felt but she didn't like how unsettling it was. She was trying to be nice, trying to reclaim the joy of being on vacation. She didn't expect to remember what she used to love about Carter, or notice how gorgeous he looked, or enjoy his company as they did things together that they once cherished. That wasn't supposed to happen. This was the Carter she remembered and loved. This Carter was grounded. Mature. Different. Phoenix hated that she liked what she saw.

When they'd returned to the resort, Carter insisted on carrying her to the room. Then stuck around and helped her get settled. The way he anticipated her needs gave Phoenix pause, leaving her heart and mind in a state of flux. Carter took charge and made sure she was taken care of. That was something else she used to love about him. He didn't seem to think about it. It happened just like when they were together, intuitively. Finally, she told him to leave. No, she insisted that he leave.

Phoenix washed the body scrub from her skin. She couldn't sit in the room all evening battling thoughts of Carter. She was going to get dressed and meet the rest of the party at Savannah and Jaxon's villa for game night even if she had to hop all the way there.

Phoenix carefully emerged from the tub, delicately

wrapped her knee and dressed as comfortably as she could. She chose a maxi dress. Grabbing her one crutch, she cautiously hobbled to Jaxon and Savannah's honeymoon villa.

Everyone was already there. Carter jumped up and met her at the door. She refused his help.

"I got it." Carter stepped aside and raised both hands in the air. Again, Phoenix didn't mean to come off so snippy. She kept doing that with him. "Thanks," she said in a softer tone as she hobbled toward a free spot on the couch. "I need to do this by myself."

"Fifi, you should be resting," Savannah said.

"I did get some rest and I took a long, hot bath." She averted her eyes from Carter. "I just wanted to get out for a bit. What are we playing?"

Ivy told Phoenix what games were played and explained what they were about to play when she came in. It was some game where they had teams and categories and each player only had seconds to come up with the answers.

"I love that game. I'm in," Phoenix said. She felt better now that she was with everyone. It didn't matter that Carter was there. Being alone with her thoughts was more troubling.

This was one game where the girls excelled, beating the guys in every round.

"How do they keep winning?" Jaxon said.

"We're smarter," Phoenix smirked, sharing high fives with the rest of the women.

Getting lost in the fun, Phoenix was able to keep her mind off Carter. Still, every now and then, when Carter would say something, she'd glance over at him and the memories would rush back. She couldn't help it. Most times she'd find that he was already staring at her.

Phoenix stayed long enough for her knee to start aching again. It was time for another painkiller and she hadn't brought any with her.

"Okay, guys. This was fun. I'm glad I came but I need to head back now. My knee is starting to ache."

"I'll walk you back," Carter said and stood.

"No!" Phoenix said fast and loud. "I mean. I'll be fine. I got over here by myself. I'll take my time."

Carter let his hands fall to his sides. "Okay, superwoman."

Phoenix narrowed her eyes at Carter. Calling her superwoman dredged up a few more memories. He used to always say that when she refused someone's help.

"I've got it." Phoenix was going to show that she didn't need assistance. She steadied one hand on the seat of the chair she was in and held the crutch with the other. She went to stand. Her knee wobbled, sending her crashing back into the chair.

Carter came to her and held out his hand. "Come on, superwoman."

Phoenix rolled her eyes at him, but took his hand. Savannah snickered. Carter wrapped his arm around Phoenix's torso to support her as she stood. She hissed from the pain once she put weight on her leg. With Carter on one side and the crutch on the other, she made her way to the door.

Everyone bid her a good-night as she and Carter left.

The walk from Savannah's villa to hers seemed to take forever. They had to stop several times to give her a moment to rest. Awkward silence filled the space between Phoenix and Carter again. Besides the pain in her knee, Phoenix's body was sore, which caused her to walk even slower.

When Phoenix and Carter finally reached her villa,

he held her as she lifted her digital bracelet to the keypad on the door. They heard the locks click. Carter pushed the door open, making way for Phoenix to take her time stepping inside. Carter hovered over her as she hobbled to the sofa and sat down.

"You don't want to go to the bedroom?"

"I'm fine here." Phoenix could have used his help getting to the bedroom, but she just wanted him to leave. His presence challenged her will again. The more time she spent around him, the less angry she was and the more she was reminded of the Carter she once loved.

"Where are your painkillers?" he asked.

"By the bed."

Carter went into the bedroom and returned with the pill bottle. He went to the mini refrigerator and grabbed a water bottle.

"Thanks!" Phoenix took the pills and washed them down with a gulp of water. When the liquid hit her stomach she was reminded of how hungry she was. She decided to order room service once Carter was gone. Meanwhile, Carter got the remote for the television and put it within Phoenix's reach.

"Need anything else?" he asked.

"Nope, I think I'm good. Thanks, Carter." Phoenix smiled. This was her attempt to dismiss him. "You can go now. I'll be fine." A second after she finished her statement her stomach growled. The sound seemed amplified in the quiet room. She looked at Carter. Carter looked at her. Another beat passed before both laughed.

"When is the last time you ate?"

Phoenix stopped laughing long enough to think about it. She twisted her lips at the thought. Consumed by the aches and pains, Phoenix forgot about eating. Her last meal was just before they rode the ATVs. “It’s been a while.”

Carter picked up the menu. “What do you want?”

“I can order my own room service, Carter. I’m fine.”

“I know. But how will you get it when they arrive with the food?”

“I’ll walk to the door and open it.”

“The same way you walked to your room? It took you ten minutes to get down the hall.”

“Ugh! Okay. Fine.” Phoenix held her hand out and Carter gave her the menu.

She flipped through and picked a few items.

“Hungry, are we?” Carter teased. Phoenix tossed one of the pillows on the sofa at him.

“Ha!” Carter swatted the pillow with a karate chop. Carter took Phoenix’s order and called it in. Picking up the remote, he turned the television on and sat on the couch with Phoenix, leaving ample space between them. They sat quietly watching Carter flip channels. “How are you feeling now, besides hungry?” Carter asked, breaking the silence.

“I’ve been better. I’ll be great when this medicine kicks in.”

“Remember when we decided to go get in-line skates out of the blue?” Carter pulled a distant memory out of the past.

Phoenix had just taken a sip of water and had to cover her mouth to keep from spitting it out after Carter’s questions. “Oh my goodness! You tumbled down that hill so fast I couldn’t keep up.”

“I was in pain for days! What made us decide to go in-line skating that day?”

“You did! I think you challenged me or something like that.” Phoenix tried to remember.

"Oh yeah. I was going to prove to you that I still had it," Carter recalled. Phoenix chuckled and shook her head. "I was wrong, but it was fun."

"You and your silly challenges. You're so competitive."

"And they were always fun, weren't they?"

Phoenix rolled her eyes. "I'll give you that."

Phoenix and Carter reminisced until her food arrived. Carter went to the door, tipped the gentleman delivering the food and laid everything out before Phoenix.

"Thanks," Phoenix said quietly. "I appreciate this." She truly did. As much as she wanted to send Carter away, his sticking around helped.

"You're welcome," Carter replied. They locked eyes. Both looked away instantly. "Um," Carter said as the mood turned awkward. "Need anything else?"

"No. I don't think so. I'm fine. Thanks for everything." She looked around, trying to avoid looking directly at Carter.

"Okay."

Neither of them moved. Carter didn't head for the door. Phoenix didn't reach for her food. Instead, she fiddled with her fingers. Carter stuffed his hands in the pockets of his linen shorts. Time slowed. Phoenix liked having him there. She didn't want him to leave but didn't dare say that. It seemed that Carter wasn't ready to leave, either. Maybe it was the painkillers kicking in.

"I guess I'll head out now," Carter said. "Let me know if you need anything."

"Yeah," Phoenix said and then the last thing she ever expected happened.

Carter bent over and kissed her forehead. "Feel better. I'll check on you in the morning." With that, he quickly walked out, leaving Phoenix spinning in her emotions.

Phoenix wanted to tell him that checking on her in the morning wasn't necessary, but she could only think about the kiss. The kiss wasn't romantic. It was caring. Normal. Familiar. It felt like something they did all the time without thinking. She watched Carter leave, clamping her mouth shut. She could feel herself getting ready to tell him to stay. She couldn't do that, especially after the kiss, even though it wasn't romantic. Still, it was a kiss. Carter had kissed her. She hadn't felt the touch of his lips in over five years. She felt another stir in her emotions, like a slow unraveling.

Ten

Carter thought about the kiss all night long. It was still on his mind when he woke in the morning. Before he knew it, he'd bent over and his lips were on Phoenix's forehead. He was surprised that Phoenix hadn't objected or pushed him away. He wasn't sure why he'd done it. Yet, it felt natural.

Carter made it his business to try and work cordially with Phoenix, even though she had been snippy. He understood. He hadn't wanted to partner with her in this wedding any more than she wanted to walk with him. How ironic was it that he was supposed to walk with her down the aisle and they had never made it down the aisle of their own wedding? When Jaxon first asked, he felt like karma was playing a cruel joke on him.

This vacation was supposed to take his mind off his issues, not add to them. Yes, they were two mature adults but so much had transpired in their past, Carter wasn't sure how this would turn out. He anticipated that Phoenix wouldn't be happy about the matchup. What he didn't anticipate was remembering how much fun it was to hang out with her. He didn't expect to notice her beauty or enjoy the sound of her laughter. He didn't expect to feel the need to run to her aid when she had the accident. Something shifted in him when he saw Phoenix's body fly off that ATV. The fall scared Carter and he didn't want to see her hurt. He had once loved the woman. Somehow, he felt like he was supposed to be there for her.

Jaxon and Savannah had another full day of activities planned for the bridal party. Phoenix would have to sit this one out. There was no way she'd be able to endure water sports. She could get the rest she needed and join them for the yacht party later that evening.

Their parents and the rest of the guests were due to arrive throughout the day. Phoenix would need her rest to be able to participate in the wedding the next day.

Carter decided to stop by her villa before heading to the lobby to meet the others. Savannah was coming out of Phoenix's door when Carter got there.

"What's wrong, Savannah?" Carter asked.

She huffed. "Phoenix. I feel bad."

"Something happened?"

"No. Phoenix is in no condition to join us today. I told her I was going to stay and help her get around today. She insisted that I join the rest of the party as planned and practically told me to get out so I could go have fun, but I'm going to stay back and help her out anyway. You should see her hobbling around that villa. Jaxon can handle the group without me."

"Savannah. You're the guest of honor. You have to go."

"I can't. I need to be there for my sister."

"I'll stay back. I can help her if she needs anything. She can call me."

"No, Carter. I couldn't ask you to do that."

"I helped her out last night. I can help her today. Besides, I could use a day to just chill. There's plenty to do here at the resort. I'll see you at the yacht party tonight."

"Really? You'd do that for me? For Phoenix?"

"Believe me it's not a big deal. I'll be close by in case she needs someone. Go have fun."

"Are you sure, Carter?"

"Absolutely sure. Enjoy yourself. You've got a big day tomorrow."

Savannah wrapped her arms around Carter and hugged him tightly. "Thanks, Carter."

"No problem."

Savannah went to walk away and turned back. "Between you and me. I was really happy to see you and Phoenix getting along yesterday."

Carter smiled. "Me, too."

"Thanks again, Carter."

"You're welcome."

Savannah headed in the direction of the lobby. Carter turned and knocked on Phoenix's door.

"Savannah!" Phoenix yelled from the other side of the door. "I told you I don't need a babysitter."

"It's not Savannah," Carter said.

"One sec," Phoenix said.

Carter waited several moments, imagining Phoenix limping toward the door. Finally, the door creaked open slowly. Carter stepped in as Phoenix headed toward the couch and plopped down.

"How are you feeling?"

"Blah."

"No jet-skiing today?" Carter teased.

"I could go if I wanted."

"Yeah, right. Superwoman is at it again." Carter sat on the couch next to her. Phoenix laughed. "I'm resting up so I can carry out my maid of honor duties tomorrow."

"Good."

Phoenix looked at her cell phone and turned her attention to Carter. "Shouldn't you be in the lobby with the rest of the group? The shuttle bus is scheduled to leave in a few minutes."

"I'm not going."

"Carter!"

Carter held his hand up. "I volunteered to stay back so your sister could go."

"No! You don't have to miss the action because of me. I'm a big girl and can handle myself." Phoenix struggled to stand. "Go on with the rest of them."

"My decision has been made. I'm sticking around. If you need anything I'll be right here."

"In my room?"

"If you want me to. After yesterday I could use a day to chill."

"No. Carter. I don't need you to do this."

"You don't have a choice. I'm sticking around."

"Ugh!" Phoenix's grunt was loud. It filled the open space.

Carter stood and walked to the sliding door and opened it. The sound of the waves crashing against the shore filled the room. He took a deep breath, taking in the salted air. Carter closed his eyes.

"This is good for both of us. I've been on the go since my plane touched down. Now I can actually sit back and enjoy the view." Carter turned back toward Phoenix. "Have you had breakfast?"

"No. I was just about to head to the dining room."

"Feel like walking? I can get it for you or we can

order room service and you can enjoy breakfast right on your patio."

Phoenix took a moment to respond. "I'd rather get out of this room for a bit."

"Say no more." Carter picked up the phone in the villa and called for a golf cart to come take them to breakfast. "Your chariot will arrive in several minutes," he said, holding out a hand as a servant would with their queen.

At first, Phoenix narrowed her eyes at him. "I don't know who's worse, you or Savannah! Help me up so I can get my things."

Carter helped her to her feet and watched as she slowly walked to the bedroom. Carter continued watching as Phoenix stuffed a towel and a book in a straw beach bag. She slid a pair of shades over her eyes. As she walked back toward the living room, he noticed she had on a swimsuit with a long cover-up that flowed in the slight breeze behind her. Carter took a breath. Phoenix looked both sexy and regal. The hotel attendant tooted the horn outside her villa. Carter held the door open so she could take her time getting through it.

Breakfast was outside overlooking a different part of the ocean. Initially, both Carter and Phoenix remained silent. Soon after, they engaged in small talk about how delicious their meal was. Like the day before, they were laughing and talking as if there wasn't a heartbreaking history between them. Carter was intrigued at how easily they slipped into comfortable banter. He thought about his conversation with Jaxon. Now that he and Phoenix were speaking, he wanted to let her know how sorry he was about what happened between them. He wanted her to know that his intent wasn't to hurt her. He was just trying to do the right thing. He may not have this opportunity again and decided to have that conversation today. Carter needed to get it off his chest but the timing had to be right. *Would the timing for that subject ever be right?* Carter thought.

"So what were you planning on doing today?" Carter asked, sipping orange juice.

"Lie on the beach. Enjoy some cocktails. Read. Bathe in the sun. It's a welcome respite after being so busy with all these excursions."

"Okay. After breakfast I'll walk you over to the beach and leave you alone to enjoy your book. If you need anything just call or text me. I won't be far so I can check on you."

"What are you going to do?" Phoenix said, placing her fork down. She pushed her plate back and rubbed her stomach.

"Not sure yet. I'll see what they have going on around here."

"Well..." Phoenix stopped talking abruptly.

"Well, what?"

"You're welcome to join me on the beach for a drink."

Carter nodded. "I think I will."

They finished breakfast and found a spot on the beach to lounge. Carter ran back to the room and changed into swimming trunks. It was as relaxing as he had expected. Phoenix read while Carter swam a few laps and took a ride on a rented Jet Ski. He didn't venture far into the water and kept his eye on Phoenix. By early afternoon they'd shared several cocktails, taking off any remaining edge as they lounged in the tropical sun.

Phoenix lifted her empty cup and the waitress taking their orders nodded. She would soon arrive with a fresh drink for her and Carter. "This is just what I needed," Phoenix said. "And this—" she held up her cocktail "—is why I skipped the painkillers this morning." She lifted her face toward the sun. "I wish I could stay here all month. There's so much waiting for me back home."

Carter groaned. "You, too?"

"Yes. Work, home, everything."

"That and more. My partner and I are starting a new venture. We're waiting on a few pieces of the puzzle to fall into place before we can launch."

"That's great news, Carter. Sounds exciting. Congratulations."

"It is. Thanks."

Phoenix sat up and looked at him. "You don't sound excited. What's up?"

"I am. I'm not looking forward to telling my father about leaving the company."

"He doesn't know yet? Yikes!" Phoenix sat back.

"His dream was for his sons to take over the business. He won't be happy. There are a few other big decisions awaiting my return. Oh, and the girl I was dating broke up with me the night before I left to come here. She basically said I was allergic to commitment. She's the second or third one this year."

"Ha!" Phoenix covered her mouth to keep her drink from spraying all over her and Carter. "Sorry. I shouldn't have laughed at that. I know a little something about your commitment allergies."

"Really, Phoenix?" The way she laughed made Carter laugh, too.

"That was cynical but funny!" Both chuckled this time. "To be honest, I probably shouldn't laugh at you. Your life sounds a lot like mine. Two days before I left, my boss told me my company was moving to the Bay Area and remote work won't be an option. How do they expect us to uproot our entire lives and make a decision to follow them across the country in a matter of weeks?"

“Whoa! Are you going?” Carter asked, suddenly alarmed by the fact that she might be moving. He had to tell her now or he’d never get the chance.

Phoenix slowly shook her head. “I really don’t know. My dad needs surgery and my mom is going to need us to help with his recovery. I want to be here for them but the opportunity to move comes with a lot of perks. I don’t want to leave New York but I hate to miss out on a great opportunity. I need to give my boss my answer within thirty days. It’s just so sudden.”

“Wow.” Carter sipped his drink.

“Oh. And the guy I was seeing isn’t so happy with me, either, so that’s pretty much over.” Phoenix chuckled. “I guess I have some commitment allergies of my own.”

“Who would have thought!” Carter chuckled, feeling a bit relieved by her admission.

“Phoenix.” Carter’s tone was serious, devoid of the teasing lightness from moments before.

“Yes, Carter?”

This was his chance. He searched his mind for the right words. “I had a baby on the way.”

Phoenix scrunched her face. “What?”

“That’s why I called the wedding off.”

“No! We’re not doing this.” Phoenix sat up and swiped her arm across her body as if cutting Carter’s words off. She reached for her beach bag.

Carter swung his leg over the side of his lounge chair and faced her. “Please.” He gently grabbed her wrists, stopping her from tossing more stuff into the bag.

“No!” Phoenix twisted her arms from his grasp. “That was the past.”

“Please! You should know. Before we got back together and decided to get married, I was dating Taylor.” The words came in a rush. Carter knew he only had minutes to get this out. "The week of our wedding, she came to me—pregnant. She was sure it was my baby. I was sure it was mine. The timing made sense."

"I don't want to hear this." Phoenix shook her head.

"You deserve to know. I didn't love Taylor, but I wanted to do the right thing and be there for my child. It was the hardest decision I ever had to make in my life. I did what I thought was best for everyone involved."

"Well, where's this baby now, Carter? Huh? Ugh!"

"It turned out not to be mine. It was months later when I found out. I'm sorry." Carter watched Phoenix shake her head. "I'm sorry," he said again. "I've wanted to say that to you for years. I never meant to hurt you." Phoenix blinked rapidly. Carter felt like he was breaking her heart all over again. He didn't mean to. He just wanted to finally tell her the truth and get past it. The damage had already been done.

Phoenix's mouth fell open. "I need to go." She ambled her way to her feet, tossed her bag across one shoulder and steadied her crutch under the other. Carter stood to assist her. She held out her hand to stop him. "No. I don't want your help."

Holding both hands in the air, Carter stepped back and let her go. He watched her as she carefully disappeared into the lobby. Carter wanted to walk her to the room, but knew she needed a moment. He would check on her later, if she allowed.

Carter hadn't expected the conversation to go well, but knew he had to tell her. After carrying that information around for years, he felt lighter now. He meant it when he told Phoenix that she deserved to know. He needed her to know.

Eleven

Phoenix avoided Carter for the rest of the day. Instead of sitting on the beach, she lounged on her balcony, taking in a more private view of the water. The rest of their family and friends were due to arrive at the resort by the evening, but Phoenix decided to remain low-key to deal with her emotions. She listened to music, ordered lunch and read her book, but none of that would take her mind off what Carter had revealed.

"Dammit!" Phoenix grunted as the thoughts took over her mind once again. She put her book down on the small table next to her lounge chair. She'd been reading for at least twenty minutes and had no idea what she'd just read. Her mind was on Carter. Why did he have to tell her all this now? Pregnant. It was a pregnancy that ended their engagement. How interesting. This was too much for Phoenix to bear.

Phoenix remembered Taylor. She was the one constant during her and Carter's on-again, off-again relationship back in college. It was as if she waited for them to break up. Days later Phoenix would see Taylor hanging off Carter's arm somewhere on the campus. Carter's dating Taylor wasn't the problem. It was the pregnancy.

Tears fell from Phoenix's eyes. She swatted them away. Carter's admission had torn open old wounds. Why did he have to bring that up? She was growing comfortable with the idea of walking down the aisle at her sister's wedding with Carter. The tension had melted away and Phoenix had actually started to enjoy Carter's company. Now she wasn't so sure.

Phoenix poured a glass of the wine she'd ordered and sat back to take in the evening sun. The beauty of the sky with its spectacle of lights should have brought her joy. It didn't. Phoenix huffed.

At least Phoenix now had the answer she'd avoided for so long. Her heart had broken into pieces the night he called the wedding off. And now it was breaking all over again. Back then she didn't want to hear what he had to say because no explanation would have made a difference. After he'd said he couldn't marry her the night before the ceremony, there was nothing else she needed to hear from him. Scenes from that night flashed before her. She'd gone from shocked to angry. Phoenix had pushed him. She screamed, cursed and told him to get out of her sight. She shouted that she hated him and that she never wanted to see him again. A few times after that she wondered what would make Carter do that to her and always arrived at the same conclusion. It didn't matter why he did it. What mattered was *that* he did it.

The days following were the worst days of her life. They were supposed to honeymoon in Belize. She went alone but hardly left her room at the resort. The solitude was what she'd needed. Savannah, her mother and friends tried to talk her out of going. When they couldn't, they decided to go with her. She insisted on going by herself. In Belize she hadn't had to answer anyone's questions about why the wedding had been called off. She couldn't tell that story one more time.

So many painful memories flooded her thoughts. New emotions battled with old ones. After the breakup she was angry and then numb. Now she was confused. This news changed so much and now her heart ached all over again. She tried not to be angry with herself.

It made sense that Carter hadn't wanted to embarrass her. That was what she would have expected Carter to do. He was a stand-up man even when he was running around college trying to be the most eligible bachelor of the campus during their breakups. It wasn't hard. Carter had always been gorgeous with his smooth brown skin, dreamy eyes and athletic build. All the Blackwell boys were charmers. Girls would dote all over them and be jealous of any other girl who seemed to hold their attention for a few weeks at a time.

A barrage of what-ifs came to mind. What if they had talked things out that fateful night? What if she had known about the pregnancy then? What if Phoenix had told him her secret? Things would have been different. They might have been married. Maybe not.

"Ugh!" Phoenix shook her head as a fresh batch of tears fell. She had to stop her mind from going back. None of those what-ifs mattered now. She'd made her decision then. It was too late now.

Phoenix had spent the better part of her afternoon reeling about the news Carter had dropped on her. Now evening was approaching and the yacht party would start soon. She needed to get herself together. There would be no excuse for her missing it. But this news was heavy on her heart and mind.

Phoenix took one last sip of wine and headed to the shower. Setting her phone to her favorite pop music playlist, she washed the leftover sand from her body, oiled her skin and put on another sundress. This time it was soft pink. She brushed her tresses, stuck her feet into comfortable flat sandals and considered herself ready. Phoenix checked her reflection before leaving her room. She didn't want to look like she'd been crying.

Phoenix dabbed on some makeup to freshen her appearance. She wished she had eye drops to reduce a bit of the redness. Looking at herself in the mirror, she smiled. It was practice for when she got together with the rest of the bridal party. The smile was to push back the pain. To make her appear happy. To hide the emotions bubbling to the surface. To keep her from falling apart. Phoenix blinked back a new threat of tears. She looked into the mirror again, staring directly into her eyes. She smiled once more, then took a deep breath.

When Phoenix stepped out of her villa, she saw Carter coming her way. A rush of air swirled in her lungs. She took three quick breaths. The last quivered as she released it. She'd prepared for being in front of everyone. She hadn't prepared for seeing Carter's face. Phoenix bit on the inside of her lip and then forced herself to smile. That smile covered a multitude of emotions.

"Hey," Carter said when he approached.

"Hey," Phoenix said back.

"I just wanted to make sure you got to the boat okay."

"Thanks." Phoenix leaned on her crutch and started walking. "It's actually better now. There's not as much pain." Her tone was tight and her words short. Phoenix thought about how ironically the pain seemed to move from one place to another, from her knee to her heart. "I'll be fine. You can go ahead."

"I'll just give you some space, superwoman."

Why did he have to say that? When he said it before today, it was funny to her. It brought back cute memories. Now it was like pouring verbal salt into her open wound. She hated feeling so vulnerable.

"Fine."

True to his word, Carter walked several feet behind her. Lincoln caught up with them by the time they reached the area where they were to dock.

"Hey, y'all! Up here!" Savannah was waving from the top deck.

Savannah looked so pretty in her white halter dress and her hair flowing in the breeze. Jaxon stood beside her as handsome as could be with one arm around Savannah's waist. They looked perfect together. Phoenix smiled for real this time. Her sister was so happy. She would use Savannah's joy to get her through the night. It was contagious.

By the time Phoenix approached the stairs, Carter was behind her, making sure she made it up without incident. Once she got onto the deck, everyone cheered.

Savannah hugged her. "You made it!" When Savannah pulled back she stared into Phoenix's eyes. "You okay?"

Phoenix grinned and shook her head. "I'm fine."

"You sure?" Savannah asked. Phoenix avoided Savannah's penetrating stare. After another moment Savannah asked, "Any pain?"

"Actually, I feel much better. I think I really needed the rest."

"Great! You don't have to move around much. Just try your best to have a good time, okay?"

"I will."

Jaxon and the others came over and checked on Phoenix, as well.

"Thanks everyone, but this party is about my sister and her dapper hubby-to-be here. I'm good. Where's the food?"

"That's my sister." Savannah laughed.

Phoenix stole a glance in Carter's direction. He was looking right at her. She wondered what he was thinking. Did he know she'd been crying? At that moment they went back to cautiously avoiding each other like they had when they first arrived in Fiji. Phoenix needed to get through the party and the wedding so she could return to her life and forget all about Carter and the what-ifs of the past five years.

Twelve

Carter wasn't sure how to take Phoenix's distant behavior at the yacht party. She didn't speak and barely looked his way. He hadn't expected her to take the news with a hearty smile, but didn't expect her to be this upset. He thought she was over it. The timing was right. They were finally speaking. No one else was around and once they got back to the US, there was no telling if he'd ever get another chance to tell her.

Carter's mind drifted to the past. His decision to walk away from their engagement wasn't easy. He'd tried to figure out better ways to handle the situation. He knew it would hurt her. That was the last thing he wanted to do. Taylor, the woman who claimed to be carrying his child, was fun to be with and always made herself available to Carter. But he didn't share the same history with her as he had with Phoenix. He met Taylor while they were in college. She was also from New York and stayed on campus at the same university as Carter and Phoenix. They'd dated off and on in college and occasionally during grad school. Their relationship hadn't been as serious as the one he'd shared with Phoenix.

Carter had had a crush on Phoenix since middle school. They finally started dating in high school. He knew then that one day she'd be his wife. But first, he needed to get his wanton lust for girls out of his system. He and Taylor ended their fling just before Carter and Phoenix reunited. They got back together in the spring before finishing graduate school, decided to marry and scheduled their wedding for that same summer. Then Taylor showed up pregnant. She was several months by then with a noticeable bulge.

Carter wrestled with his emotions for months after the cancellation. He found it hard to eat and lost weight. He buried his pain and focused on Taylor, doing everything he needed to do to be there for her and their baby. Carter didn't love Taylor, but still put in the effort to make a relationship work. His father said it was the right thing to do. He figured he might grow to love Taylor. Most of all, he wanted to be there for his child. Blackwells weren't deadbeat dads.

Carter had accompanied Taylor to doctors' appointments, made midnight runs for ice cream, rubbed her aching feet at night and shopped for baby furniture. Pride filled his chest when the doctor announced they would be having a boy. Despite moving forward with Taylor, they maintained a low profile around his family. His mother, who always had a sixth sense about things, never took to Taylor. Carter figured his family was used to Phoenix and would soon adjust, especially once the baby came.

At his mother's insistence, Carter requested a DNA test shortly after the baby's arrival. He had found out the baby wasn't his. He was furious and let Taylor know exactly how he felt without mincing words. Carter was also torn. He had gotten used to life without Phoenix and settled into the idea of having a son with Taylor. He loved the child before he was born and was instantly smitten with his big brown eyes the moment he entered the world. He bonded with that baby boy and was crushed a month later when he learned he wasn't the father. He was crushed again after learning that he didn't have to wait until the baby was born to confirm that it wasn't his. The woman who'd administered his DNA test told him he could have found out as early as nine weeks into Taylor's pregnancy. Carter wouldn't have had to call off his wedding. He had to live with the decisions he'd made.

"What's on your mind, bro?" Lincoln's voice pulled Carter from his bitter memories. He handed Carter a drink.

Carter sighed. "Too much," he said as he took the drink from Lincoln and sipped.

"This is the life," Lincoln said, leaning on the railing as he and Carter faced the setting sun.

"It is! Cheers." Carter lifted his glass to Lincoln for a toast.

"Wanna talk about it?" Lincoln asked.

"Not now."

"Okay. Phoenix seems to be doing better. That was scary," Lincoln said, referring to Phoenix's incident. He shook his head. "I'm glad it wasn't worse."

"Yeah. She's a tough one. Always has been," Carter reminisced.

"Come on. Join the party. You've been over here looking like your dog died long enough," Lincoln said and laughed at the common phrase his family used to describe when someone seemed down.

"Ha! Whatever, bro. You're right, though. I just have a lot on my mind. I need to get back to the party."

The two of them walked over to where the rest were dancing, chatting and nibbling on hors d'oeuvres. Carter checked his demeanor on the way.

"Welcome to the party, cousin-in-law," Savannah announced. "Glad you decided to join us."

"Yeah, Carter. What's up? You act like your dog died," Ivy teased.

That got Carter laughing again. "Lincoln just used that on me."

"Ha! That's a Blackwell for you," Ivy said.

He glanced at Phoenix and averted his eyes before she or anyone else could catch him looking. "Just a lot on my mind. And that water is mesmerizing. Did I miss anything good?"

"Just Jaxon's silly jokes. I see why he's marrying Savannah. She actually laughs at them," Ivy said.

"That's my baby!" Jaxon said, squeezing Savannah in his arms. It was evident that the cocktails he'd been consuming were working on him.

"We might need to turn the party up a notch." Carter walked away to ask one of the attendants if they could turn the music up and play one of his favorite songs.

The popular melody sailed through the deck and everyone jumped to their feet to dance, except Phoenix. She danced from her chair, raising her crutch in the air to the rhythm of the party tune. The rest of their time on the water was filled with good music, dancing and the group reminiscing about their favorite songs. By the time the boat docked, most of them were in high spirits from the drinks and the fun they had. Carter had almost forgotten about his worries until he saw Phoenix struggling to get down the stairs. It seemed that everyone expected that he'd be the one to help her along.

Phoenix didn't object this time. Yet, she still hadn't spoken to him. Quietly, he proceeded to walk her to her villa. The awkwardness that initially settled between them was back. Only this time it was accompanied by a thick tension. The walk seemed longer. Both cleared their throats several times.

"Listen." Carter broke the silence when they reached her door. "I didn't mean to upset you."

"Don't worry about it." Phoenix cut him off, held her wrist up to the door and turned the knob.

"I thought the timing was right. We were getting along and..."

"It's evident you still have an issue with timing," Phoenix snapped.

Her comment stung. Carter took a deep breath and exhaled slowly. He tried not to lose his patience with her. "Fine," his tone was even. He took a step back, adding space between them.

"I'm sorry. I shouldn't have said that." Phoenix carefully stepped over the threshold and turned back toward Carter.

"I'm sorry, too," he said. "Hopefully, we can move on. It was nice being friendly. Maybe one day we could go back to that."

Phoenix looked away. When she looked back at Carter there was something unreadable in her eyes. Had she been more affected by his news than he realized? Their eyes locked. Carter felt himself moving closer to her.

"We just need to get through the wedding tomorrow and the next few days and we can go back to living our normal lives. You won't have to see me and I won't have to see you."

"You're right," he said outwardly. Inside, he didn't like the idea of never seeing her again. The past few days awakened something in him. Even the tense moments reminded him of what they once shared.

Carter kept his eyes on hers. She held his gaze. Old feelings returned, stirring his emotions. Perhaps those feelings never left and remained dormant in his soul. His heart quickened. Desire flooded him and he wondered what Phoenix would do if he kissed her. She still hadn't looked away. Was she waiting for him to leave? Did she want to kiss him as much as he wanted to kiss her? Maybe she was having some of the same crazy thoughts. Maybe old feelings were coming to the surface for her, too.

Carter stepped closer to Phoenix. She didn't move. Carter noticed the rise and fall of her chest become more intense. He stepped closer. She stayed put. He watched her throat shift as she swallowed. He smelled the sweet scent of perfume. He wondered if he could taste the salt on her skin.

Carter wasn't sure what he was feeling, but he felt something. It was more than lust, despite the horrible timing. He missed Phoenix. The thought of her absence burned in him. In this moment he realized every woman since her was an attempted replacement. That was why none of those relationships worked. But Phoenix would never have him. Would she?

Random thoughts flashed in his mind. What if Taylor was never pregnant? What if he had known the baby wasn't his before calling off the wedding? Did he still want Phoenix? In this moment he did.

Carter closed the space between them so tightly he could feel her breath. He brushed her cheek with the back of his fingers and whispered, "I'm sorry."

Phoenix closed her eyes and a tear fell.

Something quickened in Carter's chest. Her tears weakened him. Why was she crying? He wanted to take care of whatever caused her to cry. He wiped her tear, leaned forward and kissed the wetness that it left behind. Phoenix stiffened slightly. He kissed her cheek once more. Carter wanted to kiss her again and again. She didn't move but hadn't objected. Carter wanted to be with her. The feeling overwhelmed him. He kissed her again. This time closer to her lips.

He gently placed his hands behind her head and pulled her to him. "I'm sorry," he whispered again, brushed his lips against her nose and rested his forehead against hers. He felt the heaviness of her pain in her breath. He longed to be her salve. Carter couldn't seem to pull himself away. He felt compelled. He craved Phoenix, wishing he could erase the past and rewrite it.

"I wish it never happened." His desire for her consumed him with heat. He pulled away to gather himself. He looked into her eyes. More tears fell. He hated seeing her cry.

Carter kissed the new tears. He felt Phoenix's body relax. She sniffled. He wished he never caused her pain. He kept kissing her, finding his way to her lips. Phoenix opened her mouth, hesitantly at first. Then she received him fully, passionately, hungrily. She invited him in. Carter's eyes closed, elated by her acceptance. Phoenix kissed him back with an urgency that matched his. When their lips parted, both were breathless.

"I'm sorry." This time Carter apologized for taking liberties even though she hadn't objected. Inside he was a happy man. The kiss was a breakthrough. He couldn't believe his thoughts. He wanted Phoenix but didn't realize how much until that moment. But was that even possible?

"Stop apologizing," she whispered, out of breath.

This time she reached for him. Carter happily obliged, kissing her passionately. The welcome feel of her soft lips almost sent him over the edge. Together they hobbled in the door enough to be able to close it. Carter felt his erection stiffen and pulled away. Phoenix looked down. He knew she felt it, too.

Carter didn't want to push Phoenix too far. If the door to her heart was opening, he needed to enter with care. Phoenix's heart wasn't something to play with. Neither was his. They had been through too much.

"I'd better go."

Phoenix gnawed on her kiss-swollen bottom lip. "Yeah. Maybe you should go." Her voice was low.

Carter wanted to pull her in for another kiss, pick her up and carry her to the bed. He restrained himself, willing his desire to be curtailed. "Good night, Phoenix."

"Good night, Carter." Her words came out in a whisper.

Carter backed out, keeping his gaze locked on Phoenix. When he cleared the doorjamb, she closed it slowly.

Thirteen

Phoenix woke in the morning to a bright sun shining down on her in the bed. She was in a haze, wondering if her memory served her right; if she really had kissed Carter the night before.

After closing the door on Carter last night, Phoenix leaned against it. She'd stayed there listening until she finally heard Carter walk away. She'd been glad when he did. It had taken everything for her not to open that door back up and invite him into her bedroom.

Carter had just kissed away her tears. And she'd let him. She was convinced that she was over Carter. Being around him these past few days had softened her resolve. Now she wasn't sure about that at all. His kiss soothed her soul and lit a fire inside her. It felt right and it shouldn't have. She yearned for more. What was she to do now?

Phoenix's tears surprised her. She never meant to cry in front of him but couldn't help herself. She'd believed him when he said he was sorry. His apology made all the feelings and memories from earlier that day come rushing back. The what-ifs returned, too. So many things could have been different had she calmed down enough to let him explain that night.

Phoenix huffed. She had to stop thinking about Carter. She was scheduled to meet her family for breakfast. The rest of the guests arrived between yesterday evening and this morning. There was so much to do to get ready for the wedding. A wedding where she would have to walk down the aisle arm in arm with Carter Blackwell. A part of her couldn't wait to see him while another part of her dreaded being in his presence because of how he made her feel.

Phoenix put her crutch aside and walked cautiously to the bathroom. Her body didn't ache as much as it had before. She'd gotten much better at walking without the crutch as long as she wasn't too tired.

Phoenix focused on getting dressed but her thoughts kept going back to Carter. "Ugh!" Those kisses were going to increase the level of awkwardness during the wedding.

What would it be like when she saw Carter? How would she feel?

Phoenix called to see if her parents and Savannah were ready. At breakfast their mom, Nadine, fussed over Savannah. She couldn't contain her excitement about her daughter's wedding. Their dad, Christopher, sat back and smiled broadly.

"I have something to tell you, Mom," Savannah said.

"What is it, sweetie?" Nadine said, reaching for her flute of mimosa.

Savannah cast Phoenix a quick glance before blurting out, "Savannah is walking with Carter in the wedding."

Their dad, Chris, sat straight up and sighed. Nadine paused with her glass midway to her mouth. "What did you just say?"

Savannah rushed to explain. "Ethan couldn't make it. Zoe is in the hospital and you know how close Jaxon is to his cousins..." Savannah continued speaking but Nadine's eyes were on Phoenix.

"Phoenix," Nadine said, calmly putting her glass down.

Savannah stopped talking. It seemed like everything stopped moving when Nadine said Phoenix's name.

"Yes, Mom?" Phoenix thought about her and Carter's kiss and felt like she was about to be scolded. Nadine had been especially upset after the wedding was called off. In fact, she stopped speaking to Carter's parents for a while until she got over it.

"How do you feel about that?" Nadine asked.

"I'm fine with it. Carter doesn't bother me. It's not like I didn't know he would be in the wedding. Jaxon is like his best friend." Phoenix shrugged off Nadine's concern.

"You sure?" Nadine eyed her skeptically.

Phoenix tried not to squirm. "Yes, Mom." She smiled. "I'm fine."

"If you say so." Nadine picked up her glass and finally sipped her mimosa.

"Are you sure, baby girl?" Christopher asked again.

"Yes, Daddy. I'm sure." Phoenix smiled, hoping it would convince him. She could never tell them about the thoughts she had about Carter. They would think she had lost her mind. They didn't know what she knew.

Christopher and Nadine looked at each other and then back at the girls.

After breakfast everyone met in one of the hotel's conference rooms to greet the rest of their family and friends. Phoenix, Savannah, Maya and Ivy went for a spa visit to get their hair and nails freshly done for the wedding. Phoenix's villa was the designated bridal party's headquarters. After the spa the girls met there with their dresses and accessories as they got dressed and helped Savannah prepare for her big day. Savannah flopped on the couch and gushed about how excited she was to become Mrs. Blackwell.

"If it were okay with Phoenix, I might try to become a Blackwell, too. That Carter is a catch."

"Maya!" Savannah chided.

"Well, Phoenix acts like she couldn't care less about Carter but I've seen the way he looks at her. I caught you tossing a few looks his way, too, Phoenix."

"I wouldn't get into that if I were you," Ivy said. "There's more history there than you know."

"Well, he already shut me down gently." Maya scrunched her face. "He's such a gentleman. I doubt he'll stay single long."

"That's enough, Maya," Savannah said sternly.

"I'm just kidding, Savannah," Maya said.

Phoenix smirked. Maya's comments hadn't fazed her one bit. She of all people knew what it was like to pass on a man like Carter.

"Be careful what you wish for, Maya." Phoenix laughed.

"Yep." Ivy laughed with her. The two slapped a high five. They had made amends years ago, and this trip made Phoenix even more comfortable with Ivy. "You don't know my brother," Ivy added and clucked her teeth. "Come on, ladies. Let's get Savannah ready to marry her sweetheart!"

"'Meet me at the altar…'" Phoenix sang an old-school R & B song. The girls joined in. "'In your white dress!'"

Savannah picked up her garter belt and swung it around in the air as they sang.

"We need to play that!" Maya said and pulled out her phone. After a few swipes the song flowed from her phone.

Maya's playlist continued as they dressed. When they were done, Phoenix, Maya and Ivy looked at Savannah in awe as if they'd collectively created a masterpiece.

"Savannah! You look..." Phoenix covered her mouth. She paused to think of the right word. "Beautiful!" Tears filled her eyes.

"Absolutely stunning," Ivy said, shaking her head.

"Girl. I didn't think it was possible for you to look more gorgeous!" Maya said.

Savannah stood and spun around. She glowed in her elegant strapless gown with its sweetheart neckline. The lace dress outlined her curves and flared at the bottom with a small train in the back. Ringlets of curls cascaded down one side of her head and her makeup was flawless. Tears welled up in Savannah's eyes.

"No! No!" the girls yelled in unison and then scrambled to find tissues.

"You cannot mess up that makeup job!" Maya said.

"Suck it up!" Phoenix said. That made Savannah laugh.

Ivy wiped her tears. "It's time." She smiled at Savannah.

There was a knock on the door and Nadine stuck her head in. She gasped.

"My goodness, honey. You look gorgeous." Nadine held one hand to her heart and blinked away tears. "Oh!" she said after a moment. "I almost forgot. The photographer is here."

"Yes. Tell her to come on in." Savannah waved her hand, welcoming the petite woman.

The photographer took pictures of Savannah and staged a few shots of the girls helping her get ready. It was time for the wedding. Ivy, Maya and Nadine surrounded Savannah as they led her to the stunning beachfront area where the ceremony would take place. Phoenix went ahead to make sure everyone else was ready. Jaxon stood under a white trellis adorned with flowers. Carter stood beside him, looking more handsome than Phoenix could stand. The setting sun and mesmerizing sea were the perfect backdrop.

Phoenix gave the nod and the music started playing. Savannah and Jaxon had chosen the song "You Are" by Charlie Wilson. Nadine made her way down the aisle and was seated. Following her were Jaxon's parents, Benjamin and Sabrina Blackwell. The bridesmaids linked with their groomsmen partners and slowly made their way down the aisle with Phoenix bringing up the rear. The music changed. The attendees stood. Chris linked his arm with Savannah's and patted her hand as he fought back tears. Everything about the moment was breathtaking.

Phoenix watched her sister, whose eyes were on her husband-to-be. Jaxon looked as if he would be the next to shed tears. He held it together. The love in the air and beauty of the moment softened Phoenix's heart. She made the mistake of looking at Carter. His eyes were already trained on her, his gaze—penetrating. It weakened her. Phoenix's breath caught. Carter wouldn't take his eyes off her. She couldn't help but wonder what it would have been like if it was their wedding. Suddenly, her heart felt heavy. She fought to keep it together.

Fortunately, the ceremony was delightfully quick. It was time for the bridal party to walk back down the aisle. Air swirled inside Phoenix's chest as Carter linked her arm in his. His touch triggered a whirlwind of emotions. It also sparked warmth deep on the inside. She longed for his kisses. Phoenix steadied herself and actually counted her steps to focus on walking without falling. She was sure her injured knee would buckle. Jaxon and Savannah eventually stopped to greet their guests. That was when Phoenix realized she'd been holding her breath. She exhaled. A few more steps and she could let go of Carter. She survived. Now she just had to get through the wedding pictures and the reception.

Phoenix had fun at the reception. Their intimate group of family and a few friends got along well despite their past differences. Everyone seemed to be over the situation between her and Carter except the two of them. Phoenix sat at the dais and watched everyone else dance. She wished she could join in but after a full day she was tired and her leg was starting to ache. She'd left her crutch in the room and needed her strength to get back without it.

Phoenix watched Carter and the rest of the bridal party on the dance floor. She was no longer upset with Carter for telling her about why he'd called off the wedding and the pregnancy. Carter was right; she deserved to know. She'd secretly wondered long enough. They were now on their way to true closure. When they got back to the States, she wouldn't have to deal with it anymore. She had to admit it was comforting to know there was a real reason behind what Carter had done. She'd battled with rejection since then and was just coming to understand that it played a role in why she ran from commitment in other relationships. Maybe that would change now, though there were still loose ends.

"How are you doing?" Carter's deep voice soothed her. She looked up at him standing by her side. His effect on her was startling.

"I'm fine. It's been a long day," she said.

"You must miss being able to dance. I know how much you like it. Wanna try?" Carter held his hand out.

Her heart fluttered. Why did she feel like a girl being asked to the prom? This was Carter, for goodness' sake. Still she hesitated, thinking of what her parents would think of her dancing in Carter's arms.

"I don't think I could manage that right now." She wished she could. She wanted to have Carter close to her again.

Carter took the seat next to her. "Are you okay about last night? I didn't mean to be too forward."

"We're good, Carter."

"Okay." He sat with her for a long while.

Neither of them said much. It was a companionable silence. Phoenix felt comfortable the way she used to with him.

Once the reception was over, the girls went back to Phoenix's room to gather their stuff. She couldn't take her mind off Carter, the way he looked, how gently he handled her as they walked, and the way he sat with her while everyone else danced. He'd catered to her every whim so effortlessly. The kiss still lingered on her lips, and desire lingered in her loins. Seeing him today only amplified her renewed longing for him.

She recalled the vision of him standing at the altar beside Jaxon. Carter looked especially handsome against the beautiful backdrop of the sea. Phoenix had discreetly taken him in from his Italian shoes to his gorgeous face. The tan suit, chosen to reflect the sand, fit his taut body ridiculously well. Instead of blazers they wore vests, white shirts and ties the hue of the water. His smooth skin glowed under the brilliant colors of the setting sun. Clean-shaven and good-looking, his eyes sparkled when he looked at Phoenix. His tall stature gave him a godlike presence. She released a sharp breath.

What if she just showed up at his door tonight? What about her mother? She saw the way she looked at Carter at the wedding. Nadine was still upset at how Carter had hurt her. Phoenix could tell. Nadine didn't mess around with her girls. Despite that, Phoenix wanted Carter. She wanted him even more now. Something had been stirred in her. She wanted to feel him even if it was just one more time. Maybe it was the ceremony that was making her this way. There was something romantic about the air in Fiji. She didn't understand why the urge was so strong but she couldn't ignore it.

Phoenix thought about drawing a bath. Just as she was about to head to the bathroom, she heard a knock. She hoped it was Carter. Phoenix opened the door. Carter was leaning against the frame with a bottle of champagne in one hand and two flutes in the other. He looked sexy as hell with his hanging tie and untucked shirt.

"Tired?" he asked, his voice setting her core ablaze.

A sly smile spread across her face. She stepped aside and waved him in. Carter stepped in slowly and paused just beyond the door. Phoenix pushed it closed.

"I just wanted to check on you." Carter's voice was seductive.

"With champagne?" She chuckled. "I'm doing just fine."

The two stood before each other, with minimal space between them. Little fires ignited along the edges of Phoenix's skin. Moments passed and they said nothing yet stared into each other's eyes. It was like Carter was waiting for her to make the first move. He seemed to want her approval. Phoenix rose on her toes and kissed his lips. She closed her eyes. It felt like falling into clouds. Still holding the champagne and glasses, Carter wrapped his arms around her and held on as if his life depended on his holding her. Phoenix melted into his arms. It was exactly where she wanted to be and felt better than she imagined.

The kiss ended slowly.

Phoenix said, “How about that dance?”

Carter smiled. He put the bottle and glasses down. Pulled up a playlist on his phone and lifted Phoenix into his arms. “I wouldn’t want you to hurt yourself.” Carter danced with her in his arms.

When the song finished, he gently placed Phoenix on her feet. She took him by the hand and led him to the bedroom. Once again Carter lifted her up and delicately laid her on the bed.

“I miss being with you. This trip made me realize that,” he whispered.

Phoenix placed her hands behind his neck and pulled him to her. Carter kissed her lips and made a trail of kisses down her neck and across her bare shoulders. He helped her out of her dress.

“Are you okay with this?” he asked as she lay naked before him.

Phoenix put her finger on his lips, quieting him. “What happens in Fiji, stays in Fiji.” Phoenix unbuttoned his shirt, ran a finger down his taut chest and then reached for his belt. Carter dropped his head back. She released the erection straining against his zipper. That was his answer. Carter kicked off his pants and continued tracing her body with steamy kisses. Phoenix hissed and her back arched at his touch.

Carter went to say something else to her and Phoenix put her finger up to his lips. She shook her head. Carter seemed to understand. She didn’t want this to be complicated. She wanted him and he wanted her. In that moment that was all that mattered.

Carter slid Phoenix farther up on the bed and buried his head between her legs. He nibbled at her pearl until she flailed against the bed and grabbed handfuls of linen. Phoenix covered her mouth with a pillow and screamed into it. Her body shuddered hard and she moaned, writhing on the bed until the orgasm finally released her. Carter kissed her with her own juices. Carefully, she rolled over and took his long, hard erection into her mouth. She wanted to give him the same pleasure he'd just given her.

Carter hissed as she took him in with long strokes, pulling out when he couldn't seem to take any more. Then he hovered over her and entered her warm canal. Phoenix's breath caught. He filled her up and she snatched the sheets so hard they snapped from the corners of the bed. The sense of delight was euphoric. Phoenix met him stroke for stroke until a guttural groan rumbled through him and out of his mouth. He held Phoenix tight and drove himself deep inside her. She clenched him with her walls until his muscles convulsed. Carter squeezed his eyes shut and refused to stop stroking until Phoenix was sated. Suddenly, she began to grunt, one short grunt after the other until they strung together in one long howl. The climax claimed her ability to control her own body, causing rigid spasms to roll through. Carter entered her faster until both howled together and collapsed, spent from giving their all. Carter wrapped his arms around her. She held him back.

"Are you okay?" he asked.

"I'm better than okay. I can't believe we did this," Phoenix said.

"I'm glad we did," Carter said and traced the line of her nose. "The question is where do we go from here?"

Phoenix wasn't ready to answer that. Instead, she massaged him back to attention for round two.

Fourteen

For the past few nights, Carter had gone to bed just before dawn. He'd spent the past three nights with Phoenix. After sunbathing, hanging with their family and more activities, Phoenix would end up in his room or he would end up in hers. They would always return to their own rooms just before dawn to keep from being detected. They didn't have any discussions about what they were doing. Instead, they laughed, joked and reminisced like old times. They had always communicated well, stretching conversations all the way from literature and politics to their favorite childhood cartoons. They reclaimed that comfortable, familiar place that used to exist between them.

They enjoyed being discreetly reconnected. Carter didn't intend to push anything. He couldn't reasonably expect anything to continue between them beyond their trip. He had his hands full with life anyway. Phoenix might move across the country. Phoenix no longer hated him. That was what mattered. He'd carried the guilt of causing her so much pain for far too long. Now he could finally let that go.

Carter wasn't sure how well they were covering up their secret. He supposed his brother Lincoln may have suspected something but now that his wife and kids were in Fiji they kept him occupied.

Carter had gotten into the habit of calling Ethan and Zoe to check in on them each morning. It was night-time for them. He was always glad to hear that Zoe was in good spirits, despite being on strict bed rest. Carter grabbed his phone so he could talk with Ethan as he took a stroll on the beach to catch the sunrise.

After the call Carter continued walking along the shore. His nights with Phoenix were amazing. This would be their last one together. Carter knew it would be special. There was no telling when he would see her again once they made it back home. Despite that, he would always cherish this time with her.

Carter chuckled when he remembered her words. *What happens in Fiji, stays in Fiji.* This would always be their little secret. Carter could imagine how they would exchange knowing glances on the few occasions they would end up in the same place.

Carter continued walking for a while and eventually came across a secluded area along the shoreline. Large rocks created a small alcove. He decided to bring Phoenix there later. Her leg was much better now and she could handle the walk. Carter headed back and joined his family for breakfast in the main dining room.

"Uncle Carter!" Lincoln's son and daughter sang as they ran up to him. Carter picked them up and swung them around in the air one by one. He kissed his sister and sister-in-law on the cheek and greeted his father and brother with a handshake. He missed his mother's presence, but Lydia refused to leave Ethan and Zoe behind alone. She wanted to make sure her grandbaby made it here.

After several days of nonstop activities, Carter and his family decided that their last day in Fiji would be a relaxing one. They spent most of the day poolside enjoying drinks, eating, talking and lying in the sun. Carter was anxious for the day to end so he could spend his last night with Phoenix. He had seen her and her family during breakfast and a few other times during the day. It seemed that they had the same idea of sticking around the resort and chilling out. When Savannah, Jaxon and Phoenix did stop by and chat with them during lunch, he and Phoenix hardly exchanged glances or words. They kept their interactions friendly and general.

At nightfall Carter sat at the bar with Ivy, Maya, Angel and Phoenix, listening to music and watching people with really bad voices sing karaoke. One by one each left, leaving him and his sister behind. Ivy finally left, insisting she needed to pack to get ready for their flight the next day.

Carter headed straight for Phoenix's room, told her to grab some towels and led her along the shore by the hand.

"Can you believe us?" Phoenix giggled, leaning against his shoulder. "Savannah would die if she knew what we've been doing."

Carter faced her and brushed his finger across her chin. "And what exactly have we been doing, Ms. Jones?"

"Ha!" Phoenix threw her head back and laughed. "You really need me to spell it out for you, Mr. Blackwell?"

"No!" Carter laughed. "Not at all." He took her hand

and continued walking. “Let me know if you get tired of walking.”

“I will.”

During their silent moments Carter tuned in to the sound of the water rolling up on the shore. He watched the moonlight ripple in the waves on the surface of the water. The blackness of the horizon was eerily fascinating. Finally, they came to the area Carter had found earlier. Just as he’d hoped, there was enough light to keep the area from being too dark.

“Give me the towels,” he told Phoenix.

She pulled them from her beach bag. Carter spread them over the sand and the two of them sat side by side, facing the sea.

Phoenix leaned her head against his shoulder. “I enjoyed my time with you.”

“I’m just glad you don’t hate me anymore.”

“What?” She swatted him playfully. “I never hated you—exactly. I mean, I wouldn’t call it hate. I was hurt.”

“I know. I hated that I hurt you.”

Phoenix looked serious and turned away.

“Did I say something?” Carter wondered what it could have been.

“Oh. No. I’m… I was just thinking about something.”

“Care to share.”

“Uh…no. It’s nothing. So…what’s the first thing you’re going to do when you get back home?”

“A better question is what won’t I do. That list is shorter,” Carter chuckled. “There’s so much on my plate.”

“Preach! I’ll have a few weeks to decide about moving to the Bay Area or finding another job. I’m just concerned about my dad. I spoke with my mom and sister about it. My mother insisted I not worry and make the best decision for me. She’s actually looking forward to coming to visit if I move. All she and Savannah want to do is shop."

"I've got some major paperwork and hard conversations waiting on me back home. It almost makes me want to stay at least another week."

"Yeah." Silence settled between them. Phoenix drew shapes in the sand. "As much as I love it here, I'm ready to go home. I need to sleep in my own bed."

"There's nothing like your own space," Carter said.

"Yeah." Phoenix paused and looked out over the sea. "Everything goes back to normal."

Carter knew she was referring to this thing between them. For a moment he wondered, what if they continued seeing one another? Then he dismissed the idea almost as soon as he thought it.

"This is our last night."

Phoenix turned to him. She gently touched his chin. "Yeah. Who would have thought?"

Carter leaned toward her and covered her mouth with his. Between kisses he told her how much he was going to miss her.

Carter's hands roamed her body as he kissed her, gently squeezing her supple breasts and pulling her closer to him. Phoenix climbed over and straddled him. His erection pushed against his shorts and nestled right between her legs. Her presence summoned him to attention.

Without breaking their kiss, Carter unsnapped her bra, lifted her dress and pushed her panties aside. He fingered her jewel, making it moist and ready to receive him. Phoenix unzipped his shorts, pulled out his erection and stroked it to a level of rigidness that Carter deemed potentially dangerous. He needed to be inside her. He came prepared this time. Carter reached in his pocket, removed the foil pack and then sheathed himself. Phoenix moaned as he entered her.

Carter gently guided her hips up and down. "Are you okay?" he asked, checking in.

"Yes." Her response was breathless. Phoenix licked her lips and groaned.

Up and down, she rode the full length of his shaft, creating a sweet rhythm. He met her stroke for stroke. Carter wanted to look her right in the eyes, but hers were closed, and her head was back. Their tempo quickened. Phoenix opened her eyes. Their gazes locked. The intensity increased. They bounced against each other harder, peering into one another's eyes. Carter loved when she stared at him boldly while they made love. Phoenix held her arms around his neck tight.

She cushioned him with the walls of her canal. Carter almost howled. He wanted her to keep looking directly into his eyes. He wanted this feeling to last forever. A wave of pleasure washed over him, threatening to send him over the edge. It was too soon. Carter needed more of Phoenix. He lifted her off him, flipped her over onto her knees and entered her from behind.

"Yes!" Phoenix chanted over and over again. "Oh, Carter!" she moaned.

"Ph...Ph... Phoenix." Carter was so overtaken by pleasure, he could barely get her name out.

His impending climax threatened to send him to euphoric destinations. He removed himself again, turned Phoenix onto her back and nibbled her pearl between his lips. He licked and teased her until her body shuddered uncontrollably. Once her peak had ravaged her completely she lay in a ball, moaning, trying to catch her breath. Carter wouldn't give her rest. He wanted to please her until she couldn't be pleased anymore. He kissed her swollen lips. Took her nipples into his mouth. Licked hot trails of kisses down her torso and entered her again.

Phoenix grunted, raked her fingers down his chest. She grabbed handfuls of sand, arching her back and bucking. Carter's long, steady strokes turned urgent and wild. Soon, he grunted each time he drove himself inside her. His body tensed. His back arched. His eyes rolled back. His pace quickened. Sweet, melodic screams escaped her mouth. Guttural moans rumbled through his chest and out through his lips. His long, deep strokes turned into quick, erratic thrusts until he pushed himself inside one last time and exploded.

Carter's muscles spasmed, forcing him to buck and hold, buck and hold. He couldn't control his muscles. They tightened with a fierce grip that wouldn't let him go. At the same time Phoenix wrapped her arms around his neck and her legs around his back and pushed against him hard. Then her body bucked and spasmed, too. Her groans rode her release until she finally lay spent, and Carter collapsed on top of her. They lay there together until their heartbeats and breathing returned to a normal pace.

Then they lay on their backs, looking into the clear midnight sky, pointing out the stars to each other.

"You make me not want to leave," Phoenix said.

"We could stay one more day. Then we wouldn't have to sneak around," Carter laughed.

"I wish."

After a while Carter asked. "Ready to head back?"

"You coming to my room or am I coming to yours?" Phoenix asked.

"Whatever your pretty little mind desires."

Carter picked up the towels and shook them out. They walked back hand in hand until they got closer to the villas where their families stayed. Carter thought he saw Lincoln walking up to his room but looked the other way.

They came to Carter's room first and dipped inside to avoid the risk of possibly being seen by anyone else. Inside they showered together, washing the sand from one another's bodies. They made love in the shower and again once they hit the bed. Carter couldn't get enough of Phoenix. The feel of her drove him to the edge of a pleasurable madness. When he reached a peak with her, it took forever for the deeply sensual sensation to loosen its grip. Making love to her was more indulgent than he ever remembered.

"I can't stay all night this time. I need to pack."

"Okay. I'll walk you over."

"No. I can manage. Besides, I don't want anyone to see us."

Carter felt a shift in her demeanor. Maybe it was because this was goodbye.

"I need one more kiss." They kissed and then Carter held her for some time.

He felt himself dozing off when he heard her calling his name softly. "Carter?" It sounded like a question and the tone had completely changed. Carter was alarmed.

"What's up?" He lifted and leaned on his elbow.

"I have to tell you something."

Carter sat completely up in the bed. Phoenix swung her legs over the edge of the mattress. She sat pensively for a moment before standing. She paced a bit and then stopped. Carter noticed how she wrung her hands.

He jumped up and went to hold her. Phoenix held her hand up, stopping him.

"What is it, Phoenix?" Carter wondered if she was

having second thoughts about the past few nights. Maybe she wanted to continue seeing him. Carter wondered if that would work. He had to be ready for Phoenix. She wouldn't give him her heart twice for him to break it.

Phoenix continued pacing.

"Phoenix!" She flinched. The volume of his tone startled her. "I'm sorry. What is it that you want to say?"

Phoenix stopped pacing and closed her eyes. She inhaled long and deep. When her eyes popped open, her mouth did, too. "I was pregnant, too."

Carter was confused. "Pregnant. What? When?"

Phoenix huffed. "Carter." She spoke slowly. "I was pregnant. I was going to surprise you and tell you on our wedding night."

"Wh—! No. No. No. No. No!" Both Carter's hands waved in the air. "Phoenix, what are you saying?"

"It's time you knew. I was carrying your baby when you called off the wedding. That's why I was so angry and didn't want to hear what you had to say."

Carter felt like time had slowed down. Confused, he sat on the edge of the bed and held his head in his hands. "What are you saying? Wh…what happened to the baby? Phoenix. Wh…where's the baby?" Carter had trouble getting his words out. He couldn't breathe.

Phoenix took a while to answer. When Carter looked up to see why she hadn't spoken, he saw the tears in Phoenix's eyes.

"I…lost it." Phoenix's hands crossed her stomach as if it ached. She caught her breath. "It happened when I got back from Belize. The doctor said it could have been from the stress. I wasn't eating… I… I couldn't eat. I… I…"

Carter grabbed Phoenix and held her in his arms. She sobbed.

"I lost the baby, Carter," she repeated.

Carter didn't know what to say. His anger only subsided due to his looming sense of guilt.

"Why didn't you tell me?" he asked, still holding her.

Phoenix pulled herself out of his embrace. "You left me! The day before our wedding. You left. I let you go, because I was angry. You hurt me. You hurt me bad. I was an emotional wreck. I wanted you out of my sight. I was going to tell you when I got back from Belize. I needed to go and clear my mind. I didn't expect to lose our baby. By then you were gone. You were with Taylor. People saw you so I didn't say anything. I thought you left me for her. I didn't know she was pregnant until you told me the other day. I never knew we were both carrying your child!"

That stung. "Taylor wasn't carrying my child. You were. You were my fiancée. You were going to be my wife and you didn't tell me."

"And you walked out on me!" Phoenix shouted, stabbing the air with her index finger.

"I would have never left if I knew you were carrying my child. I could have worked something else out. Ugh! I was just trying to do the right thing." Carter stood and paced circles at the end of the bed.

The weight of all Carter had lost crushed him, making it difficult to breathe. The words scrambled in his mind and wouldn't make sense coming through his lips.

Phoenix dried her tears. Picked up her beach bag to leave. He followed her to the door not sure of what to say. She paused once she opened the door. "You had to know." The pain in her voice was evident. She softly closed the door behind her.

What was Carter to do with this information? They

had messed up and it was a cost they could never recover. Carter went back to the bedroom, lay back on the bed and stared at the ceiling.

Fifteen

Phoenix was happy to be home, but after a bad case of jet lag and the string of sleepless nights she had spent in Carter's arms before she left, she wished she could sleep twenty-four more hours but she had to go back to work. She lifted her hand and smiled at the doorman in her luxury condo in downtown Brooklyn. The older gentleman returned her customary greeting with a nod.

Phoenix hit the sidewalk and maneuvered through the throngs of people heading to work during the morning rush hour. She loved the vibe of her new neighborhood. It was alive and breathing with its own pulse. Within a few short blocks, she had access to coffeehouses, galleries, boutiques, fitness studios, poetry lounges and restaurants boasting cuisine representing every culture across the globe. Moving to Brooklyn from Long Island had shortened her commute to work significantly. Her office was a short train ride to a renovated brownstone on the other side of downtown. She even loved the noise of the city, chatter, cars, dogs barking, horns, music flowing from car windows or through the doors of coffee shops. It all synced together to create its own rhythm—a musical backdrop. It was so different from the neighborhood she grew up in on Long Island's Gold Coast, with large homes on sprawling grounds and eerily quiet, tree-lined streets.

Brent offered to pick her up at the airport when she returned but she refused, preferring a drama-free ride with the car service she'd ordered. He also reached out to her as she was stepping into work. She responded with a text, can't right now. She thought she made it clear to him that she wanted to break up before she left for Fiji. Their situation had passed its expiration date way before she ended it that night. Yet, he called and texted her several times about her not reaching out to him while she was away.

Brent texted again to say that he needed to talk to her, and asked if he could stop by after work. Phoenix wished she were back in Fiji with Carter. However, she was sure Carter wasn't too happy with her, either. She hadn't spoken to him since she left his room several nights ago after telling him about the baby. Whenever she thought back to that moment and seeing the look on Carter's face, her stomach tightened. Phoenix thought she had buried those memories and the pain that came with them. Carter reopened those wounds when he confessed his true reason for calling off the wedding. It was hard to relive that moment, but harder to reveal to Carter the secret she held for all those years. She couldn't decide whose revelation was worse, and hated to think that had she just listened to him that night or had told him about the baby, things may have been very different. She didn't know whether to direct her anger at him or herself. She had absolutely no idea what to do with the guilt she'd been feeling.

Not even her parents knew about her pregnancy. Phoenix couldn't tell them before telling Carter but then she never got to tell Carter. Savannah knew about the miscarriage. She was the one Phoenix called when she woke up to gut-wrenching cramps and blood-covered sheets. She'd sworn Savannah to secrecy back then.

Phoenix looked at the time on her cell phone. She managed to reach her office without running into anyone. She had arrived early but expected Indra and Dean to be around. Getting settled, she put on some music, turned it down low and started up her laptop. Coming back to work after being away for two weeks was wonderful, but the four hundred emails in her inbox made her wish she has checked in a few times while she was out.

A knock on her office door pulled her attention away from the emails. Indra stuck her head in and then stepped all the way into the room. "Hey! How was the trip?"

"It was—" Phoenix thought about all that had transpired, from the announcement that Carter was going to be the best man to her accident, reconnecting with Carter and things she'd learned "—part amazing, part interesting."

"You look tanned and refreshed."

"Thanks. I still haven't recovered from jet lag. If I start sleepwalking don't trip me."

"Ha!" Indra laughed. "I wanted to drop in and say hello. Dean and I have to fly out to the Bay Area for meetings. I'll be back midweek. I know you're just getting back but do you think you'll have an answer for me?" Indra tilted her head. "We'd really love for you to join us."

Phoenix felt like a belt was tightening around her chest. "I'm working on it."

"Good. Call me if you need me. We'll do a video call with the team with updates after all of our meetings. See you when we get back."

"Safe travels," Phoenix said and smiled. As soon as Indra left and shut the door, the smile fell off Phoenix's face.

Phoenix had two weeks left to make one of the biggest decisions of her life. She'd visited California a dozen times and loved it but had no interest in living there. If she didn't go, she needed to find a new job. The idea of injecting herself into the job market search was another headache she didn't look forward to.

Just then, her phone rang. It was her mother, letting her know that their father's surgery date was pushed up. She remembered how carefully he walked in Fiji. Her mother wanted everyone to make sure they were available the evening of the surgery to see their father. Phoenix made the adjustment on her calendar and her phone rang again. Phoenix cocked her head to the side and shook it.

"Hello, Brent." If she didn't answer he would keep calling.

"You didn't answer my text. I really need to talk to you tonight. Can I come by?"

She flicked her gaze upward. "Meet me at Mona's at seven."

"Thanks. See you there…" Brent paused. "I miss you."

"I have to go, Brent. See you later." Phoenix ended the call.

Brent's words didn't make her miss him. They made her think of Carter. She missed his presence. She wondered how he was dealing with the news about the baby since they'd never spoken after that. She'd been wondering since she boarded her flight back home. Carter was hurt and so was she. Phoenix wondered if the weight of their decisions to hold on to this information for so long weighed as heavily on him. She was tired of considering all the possible scenarios in her head. If they had talked, perhaps they would have been married now.

Phoenix stood and rounded her desk. She picked up her phone and dialed Savannah's number. She was the only person on whom Phoenix could have possibly unloaded all of the thoughts she'd been carrying.

"Hey, Fifi. What's up? Aren't you at work?"

Phoenix was having second thoughts about bringing up the conversation. "Yeah. Brent keeps calling me. He wants to meet." She couldn't bring herself to start the conversation about Carter. She needed more time to navigate through her feelings. Phoenix wasn't even sure where to start.

"I bet he wants you back. What are you going to do?"

"Ugh!" Phoenix rubbed her brow. "I told him I'd meet him at Mona's tonight. I don't want him coming to the house."

"Noted. If I hear of a disturbance at Mona's I'll know it's you. Hopefully, you won't have to hit him with some of the Brazilian jujitsu you've been learning." Savannah cackled loudly.

That brought a smile to Phoenix's face. "Hopefully not." There was another knock at Phoenix's door. She held the phone away from her face. "Just a moment," she said and then turned her attention back to her sister. "I gotta go. I'll let you know what happened." Phoenix walked over and opened the door. Both Dean and Indra were standing on the other side. They looked as if they were up to something. “Hey,” Phoenix said. “How can I help you?”

Dean stepped in first and then Indra. They were silent until they closed the door behind them.

“We know you’re still thinking about your decision, but we wanted to share something with you,” Dean said and glanced at Indra.

Indra jumped in. “We really want you to stay with the team. So…”

“If you decide to join us, we’d like you to run our research and development department. It will require more responsibility and of course a salary increase,” Dean said.

“We hope this will help with your decision.” Indra handed Phoenix a folder. “Please consider this offer while we’re away.”

Taken aback, it took a moment for Phoenix to take the folder from Indra. “Thanks. I’ll definitely look through this carefully.”

“That’s all we ask,” Indra said. She took Phoenix’s hand in hers. “Thanks.”

“You’re welcome,” Phoenix said. She groaned when they left. Indra and Dean were doing everything they could to convince her to go. Maybe she should give it a chance for a few months and see how it worked out. But would she be happy in California?

Phoenix spent most of her day catching up on emails. She left in time to go home to change into more casual clothing before meeting Brent at Mona’s. She chose the coffeehouse instead of a restaurant because she wanted this meeting with Brent to be as brief as possible.

As she expected, he arrived before she had. Brent waved her over to the small table by the window. It was the place she loved to sit when they went there together.

"Hey." Brent stood. He leaned forward to kiss Phoenix on the cheek.

"Hey." Phoenix returned his greeting.

Brent stood for another awkward moment with his hands stuffed in his pockets.

Phoenix sat down and Brent followed suit.

"How was your trip?"

"It was good. The wedding was nice." Carter flashed across Phoenix's mind again. He would forever be the dominant memory for her when it came to Fiji.

"Great!"

A barista came over and placed two mugs in front of them.

"I ordered you a chai latte," Brent said.

"Thanks!" Phoenix wrapped her hands around the mug. She always loved feeling the warmth of a hot drink. She took a sip. "What did you want to talk about, Brent?"

"I know I upset you before you left and you said you wanted to cut things off. I apologize for getting a little… crazy over things at times. I figured if we both had a little time to think things over, then maybe we could start fresh and give it one more try."

"Brent."

"Let me finish. I don't know why I get so crazy when I think of another man even having a conversation with you. It's just that you're a beautiful woman and I know what it's like to have someone I love taken from me."

Phoenix blinked rapidly. "Brent?"

"Yes. I said *love*. I love you, Phoenix, and I don't want to lose you. I want to give us another try."

Phoenix squeezed her eyes shut and rubbed her forehead. In her mind she saw a sea of red flags. Brent was a nice guy and very good-looking but his negative traits outweighed his good ones—the jealousy, the quick temper, comparing her to his previous relationships. He'd managed to hide these traits when they first started dating, but then the real Brent showed up. Phoenix knew none of that would change. If she said yes, she'd go back to feeling suffocated. Carter popped into her mind. She remembered how easily they got along, how they could talk for hours, how he knew her so well and how he anticipated her needs. Carter wasn't jealous. He exuded confidence. Then she wondered why she compared Brent to Carter. He had nothing to do with their relationship.

"You don't have to answer me now. I didn't want to do this by text."

"There's no need to prolong this. I'm sorry, but this is over, Brent."

He slammed his hand against the small bistro table, causing the cups to wobble. Phoenix flinched and then narrowed her eyes at him. Coffee and chai tea latte spilled over the rims. Patrons sharply turned their way. "Dammit, Phoenix. You didn't even think about it."

Brent seemed completely oblivious to the scene he caused. Phoenix's jaw clenched.

Phoenix tilted her head back and gazed upward. Then she looked at Brent for a moment. She thought about explaining how his actions were part of her reason for leaving but then realized that explaining wouldn't change the way she felt. She wanted a man that treated her like Carter had in Fiji.

"Brent. There's nothing more for me to think about here." Phoenix stood. "Thank you for the chai. Goodbye." She calmly walked out. With all that she had on her plate, there was no room for Brent's antics. She didn't bother telling him she might not be around in another month anyway.

Phoenix walked back to her apartment. Her encounter

with Brent only made her miss Carter's presence more. She wished he could sneak to her apartment and spend the night with her like he had in Fiji. But she wasn't sure that Carter would want to talk to her anyway.

Their baby would have been almost five years old. If only she had dealt with Carter differently when he came to her that night…

Sixteen

Carter thought he saw Phoenix walk into the coffeehouse next to the bodega where he got his bacon, egg and cheese breakfast sandwich from each morning. He picked up his pace, jogging to the entrance, only to realize it wasn't her. That was the third time in the week since he'd been back from Fiji that he thought he saw Phoenix in his Brooklyn neighborhood. From what he knew, Phoenix lived on Long Island. Carter was convinced that his mind was playing games with him.

He attributed these "sightings" to the trauma of knowing that he actually had a child by the woman he loved but that baby didn't make it. He walked out on Phoenix to be with a woman who lied to him about carrying his baby. It was ironic and unfair. He was angry that Phoenix withheld that information from him. The pain of losing that child that he hadn't known about felt surreal. His anger subsided when the guilt took over. Had he not canceled their wedding, maybe she wouldn't have suffered from so much stress and lost their baby. What could he do now besides torment himself with possibilities that he couldn't do anything about?

Carter had more immediate concerns. One of his investors was threatening to pull out of the deal for his new business venture with his partner and friend, Harris Cooper. He needed to figure out a way to save the deal. The money was one thing, but this investor came with connections that were critical to get their technology business off the ground. His father had just gotten on him about not being focused with work and he still hadn't told Bill about leaving. If they were able to convince this investor to stay, they would be able to get things rolling in weeks. Harris and he already had office space picked out in downtown Brooklyn.

Carter was back to the horrible sleeping patterns that he'd had before vacation. He hadn't gotten the rest he anticipated on vacation, either, especially once he and Phoenix started hooking up. Now that he was home, the workload from Blackwell Wealth Management, along with his business ventures, left him with little time to sleep.

The time with Phoenix brought so many feelings to the surface. He wished she were coming to his room tonight to soothe all the stress of work. Yet, they agreed that their time together would be over after Fiji. Too many issues were stirred with both of their admissions and after that last night, he had no idea where they stood. Despite it all, he missed her. He was angry with her. He cared about her. He was sorry for what he'd done all over again.

Carter looked at his watch. If the cook didn't hurry with his sandwich, he would end up running late. They had meetings at Blackwell Headquarters today. All the regional managers would be there except Ethan. He was still spending every day by Zoe's side at the hospital, hoping she'd be released soon and praying they wouldn't lose their baby.

Carter's phone rang. It was Harris. "What's up?"

"Roberts is out!"

"What?" Carter said loud enough for the other people in the store to look at him. He lowered his voice. "Dammit! What went wrong? Let me call him."

"I'm not sure if it will do any good," Harris said.

"I need to at least try."

"Call me back if you get him."

Carter ended the call and dialed Jacob Roberts. Roberts didn't answer. "Ugh!" Carter tried again. This time he left a message, asking for Jacob to call him back. Carter finally got his food, made his way out of the crammed bodega and headed for his train.

Carter made it to the Blackwell offices just in time. Like his father, Bill, he was a stickler for time, considering tardiness a form of disrespect. This morning's meeting was a quarterly one where they reviewed the state of the business and strategized on how they could remain on track to meet and exceed their goals in the next quarter. It required brainpower that Carter wasn't sure he could manage. He was tired, had too much on his mind and was now facing a major issue with regards to this new business. If they didn't find another investor willing to offer as much as Roberts with some of the same connections there was a chance that his business wasn't going anywhere.

His brain hurt from trying to think of how they could fill the gaping hole Roberts's departure would leave in their financial plan. This tech company wasn't a cheap start-up. They needed to invest in the best technology experts to attract the kind of business that would get them the right returns. It came at a high cost. The market research confirmed that there was a gap they could fill effectively and scale up quickly.

Carter headed into his office at the headquarters, closed the door behind him and called Harris back.

"I called a few times. He's not answering. It's early so I'll try again when we get a break," Carter told Harris.

"In the meantime, let's reach out to our other prospects," Harris said.

Carter decided to try Roberts one more time before heading to the conference room.

"Roberts!" Carter was surprised he answered.

"Blackwell?"

"We need to talk," Carter said.

"I'm not sure it will matter, Carter."

"I'm about to run into a meeting now, but I have an idea. It's a bit of a renegotiation."

Carter could hear Roberts sigh. "I'll hear you out, Carter. Noon. How's that?"

Carter pumped his fist. "Perfect. Will this number work?"

"Yep. I'll only have about an hour. I'm flying out to Seattle this afternoon so after that you won't be able to get me."

"I think once you hear what I have to say you'll be ready to jump back on board."

"We will see."

"Talk to you later," Carter said and ended the call. He wasn't willing to let Roberts go so easily. Carter was used to getting what he wanted most of the time.

Getting the meeting gave him one less thing to worry

about. Now he could focus on what was ahead of him at Blackwell.

Carter gathered his laptop and a few files but before he could make it to the door, his father, Bill, rushed into his office. “Carter, it’s Zoe!”

Carter’s stomach tightened like a rock. “What happened, Pop?” His father’s fair skin looked pale. Small beads of sweat lined his forehead. This didn’t look good.

“Ethan called. He was distraught. I could hardly understand what he was saying. We need to get to the hospital now. Your mom, Lincoln and Ivy will meet us there. I already arranged for a car.”

Carter became aware of every beat of his own heart. It thumped with fear. He said a discreet prayer as he stuffed his laptop into a bag. He could only imagine what Ethan and Zoe were going through right now. He couldn’t bear his brother and wife losing their baby.

Seventeen

Phoenix opened the folder from her bosses again and spread the contents across her desk. The offer was incredible. She loved her work. She was used to money. It was the perks that were most convincing. They offered Phoenix a huge promotion, a company vehicle, compensation for relocation services, stock options in Jabber and more. They even gave her extra time to make her decision, which would allow her to join them in California several weeks later. That took some of the pressure off. Until this point, none of the other jobs she'd applied for had called her back. She didn't want to move, but the more they sweetened the deal, the more she considered it. Maybe she could try it out for a few months and see if she'd like it. Her main concern was her father's health.

Phoenix was glad that her dad's surgery was pushed up but then they found that he had formed blood clots, which brought on a new set of concerns. Her mother tried to remain calm but Phoenix could tell from the bags around her eyes that she hadn't had any sleep. Today she was going to the hospital after work to stay with him for the evening so her mom could go home and rest.

Her parents were getting older. Savannah had a new husband. Phoenix expected to be the one to fill in for her mother when needed. She couldn't do that from California. She'd just purchased her brownstone in Brooklyn months ago and absolutely loved her new neighborhood. Silicon Valley was nothing like Brooklyn. As much as she loved traveling, she never had a desire to live outside New York. Maybe it was time she did something different, unexpected. Had Savannah been given this offer she probably would have packed up her house already. She was spontaneous and sometimes flighty. Phoenix was practical and calculated.

Phoenix left work early so she could avoid traffic on her drive from Brooklyn to Long Island. Her dad was resting when she arrived. She didn't want to wake him so she tuned in to an audiobook until he woke up.

"Sweetie," Chris's voice was groggy.

"Hey, Daddy."

Phoenix leaned over and gave him a kiss on his forehead. She pulled her chair closer and sat next to his bed. "How are you feeling?"

"I've had better days," Chris said.

"Feel like talking? You can mostly listen while I talk."

"Sure. What's on your mind?" Chris cleared his throat.

Phoenix updated him about work and explained her trepidation about moving.

"You don't worry about me and your mother. We will be fine. What else do you think is holding you back?"

"I love home. I love my new place. I'll have a few coworkers but I don't know anyone else there. West Coast living is so different."

"You're comfortable," Chris said matter-of-factly.

"Yeah. I am," Phoenix said proudly.

"And you know comfort can be the enemy of progress?"

"Oh! Yeah." She sat back in her chair.

"You just don't want to become stagnant. Then you stop growing altogether."

"I know, Dad. But does progress have to mean moving across the entire country?"

"Not at all. The options are endless. Heck! Start your own business."

"Hmm." Phoenix thought for a moment. She'd considered starting her own business in the past but not seriously. "Thanks, Dad." Phoenix's phone vibrated. Savannah's name lit up the screen.

"Hey. I'm here with Dad."

"Hey, Daddy," Savannah yelled into the phone.

There was no need to transfer the message. Though the phone wasn't on speaker, Chris heard Savannah, chuckled and said hello back.

"Have you spoken to Carter?" Savannah asked.

"Me? No. Why?"

"Jaxon just told me that Zoe went in for an emergency C-section. Ethan is completely distraught. They have to take the baby."

"Oh no! When did this happen? Why?"

"Earlier today. I'm not sure what caused it. They didn't say. I'm hoping everything turns out okay." Savannah's sigh was clear through the phone. "Jax is trying to find out more. I just wanted to let you know. Jax and I are going to go by the hospital later."

"Okay. Keep me posted."

"I will. Talk to you later. Tell Daddy I said bye," Savannah said and ended the call.

Phoenix stayed with her father a while longer before excusing herself to call Carter. She checked the family lounge. No one was there so she stepped in. Phoenix held her phone in her hand, staring at Carter's name for a while before she dialed his number. This was the first time she would hear his voice since their last night together in Fiji.

"Hello," Carter answered. His voice was listless.

"Hey. Carter. Um, I heard about Zoe. Is she okay?"

Carter cleared his throat. "We hope so. She's in surgery now. I'm here with Ethan. He's worried."

Phoenix's hand slowly went to her heart. "I pray everything will be okay."

"Me, too." Carter sounded tired.

"You sound exhausted," Phoenix said.

"Yeah."

Neither spoke for a few moments.

"I'm so sorry about all of this. Please tell them I'm thinking of them." Phoenix was generally concerned. "Would you mind keeping me posted?"

"I will." Carter paused. "Thanks."

There was a long pause. "Carter?"

"Yes?"

"Let me know if there's anything I can do for you."

"There is," Carter said.

"Oh. Okay. What is it?" Phoenix asked.

"Let me come see you tonight."

Eighteen

Carter sat in the car outside the address that Phoenix had given him on the phone. He contemplated whether or not he should go in. It was past ten at night. He had asked her if he could come by without thinking about it. She'd said yes. That surprised Carter. Messy issues resided between them but despite that, he needed her. Carter needed to feel the way he felt during those nights they'd spent together in Fiji. He knew then that it was temporary. Tonight would be temporary, too.

Carter's day couldn't have gone worse. After his father told him about Ethan and Zoe, he completely forgot to call Roberts at noon. He hoped he hadn't completely botched his chances of getting him back on board as an investor. Never had Carter had so much weighing on his mind at once. Going home to an empty house was the last thing he wanted to do.

Carter left the hospital after Zoe was out of surgery

and back in her room. She still had a long road to recovery and so did the baby. Born prematurely, their little girl was sent to the neonatal intensive care unit where she was likely to spend the next few months. When Carter had left the hospital, Ethan had fallen asleep in a chair next to Zoe's bed. They were still holding hands. Carter couldn't remember the last time he'd seen his brother cry. He could never say he understood what Ethan was going through, but the situation made him think of his own past with kids. It hurt him to walk away from the son that Taylor had told him was his. He had already bonded with the little boy. And it hurt even more when he found out about Phoenix's losing the baby and having to deal with that loss on her own.

Carter looked at his watch. It was almost half past ten. If he was going in to see Phoenix, he needed to get out of the car now. After a few more moments he pushed the car door open and headed to the lobby of her building. The slate gray and glass building looked like a work of contemporary art nestled between older structures. He told the doorman where he was headed and he guided him to her apartment.

Carter lifted his hand to knock and paused. After a deep breath he tapped lightly. Moments later Phoenix opened the door. One look in her eyes and he felt some of his burdens lighten. She was beautiful even with her hair piled on top of her head in a messy bun. He'd never seen a pair of lounge pants and a tank top look sexier. The fluffy slippers made him smile. She stepped aside and welcomed him in.

"Hi," she said.

"Hi," he said back. Carter looked around. The decor was simple, elegant, feminine and cozy. Pale gray walls were adorned with interesting colorful art. The artwork set the stage for the colorful accents that popped against the muted backdrop. A basket sat in the corner with plush throws rolled inside. One large knitted throw lay across the back of the couch.

Carter stood in the living room, several feet from the door. He still wasn't sure he'd made the right move by coming over. His mouth operated without his brain.

"Are you okay, Carter?"

He shook his head. Phoenix went to him. At first, she looked directly into Carter's eyes. She embraced him. Carter held her back. He didn't want to let go. He belonged in her arms. She looked at him once again. Time slowed. Carter gazed back at her. There was that pull again. He needed to feel her lips. Leaning forward, his lips connected with hers. Heat surged through him as well as something more primal. He needed Phoenix even if it was just for the night. Not just her body. He needed the comfort she gave him.

Carter released his passion in their kiss. He held her by the waist. Phoenix's arms were around his neck. Carter pressed his body against hers. Phoenix showed no signs of resistance. She pressed back against him. Another heat surge.

"I need you," he whispered without pulling his mouth away from hers.

Phoenix nodded, giving Carter the green light.

Carter lifted Phoenix. She wrapped her legs around his waist. Carter felt his way through her apartment and into her bedroom. He found it with ease as if he'd been there before. Gently, he laid her across the well-made bed. They tore at one another's clothes until they were naked. Carter admired her body, running a finger from the crook of her neck to her navel. He planted teasing pecks on her mouth and down her torso. They were quick and moist.

Phoenix's skin was on fire. That drove Carter's desire higher. Phoenix pulled protection from her side drawer and held it up. Carter lifted his chin. Phoenix unwrapped it and slid it onto his erection. She massaged it before lying back and letting him enter her wet canal. Carter went as far as she could take him, driving himself inside her with long, deep strokes. The intense pleasure threatened to send him over an immediate edge.

Phoenix's nails dug deep into his back. The pain brought Carter pleasure. His strokes were slow and deliberate. He watched Phoenix's face. Her eyes were closed and her mouth agape. Her expression, euphoric. Carter wanted nothing more than to please her. When she bit her bottom lip, an involuntary spasm started in his groin and spread through his lower body. Making love to her was indulgent. He wanted to stay inside her but couldn't take much more.

Carter pulled out and kissed her body from head to toe before returning, zoning in on her pearl. He buried his face between her legs and lapped at Phoenix until her legs trembled. Covering her mouth with a pillow, she released her bliss in a series of groans until her body stopped convulsing.

Just as she came down, Carter entered her again, driving her back to euphoria. This time he held her in his arms as he drove himself deep within her walls. Phoenix held him back, squeezing him tighter as she neared another climax. This time they rode the pleasure wave together, bucking and convulsing as their twin orgasms rolled through them like violent waves. Neither released their hold until their bodies stopped quaking and their breathing returned to normal.

Carter lay facing Phoenix, staring into her eyes. For a long time he basked in their afterglow, still feeling remnants of pleasure in smaller, less frequent waves.

Phoenix touched his face. "Are you okay?"

Her question jolted him. He came to Phoenix for comfort but didn't plan for them to end up in bed. Carter embraced the relief that being in her presence offered.

"I don't want you to think I just came for this."

Phoenix rolled her eyes upward. "I know. We can say that it just happened."

Carter kissed her lips again. "Thank you for letting it happen." He chuckled.

"I guess we need to talk," Phoenix said. She got up and went to the bathroom.

Carter stayed on the bed, folding his hands behind his head. He thought about his day. He was glad he came. He thought about the talk they needed to have and felt some trepidation.

Phoenix returned to the room with a robe on and two glasses of wine. She placed the one for him on the dresser while Carter took his turn to freshen up.

When Carter came out of the bathroom, Phoenix was on her balcony. Carter slipped into his slacks and put on his shirt, leaving it unbuttoned, and then joined her outside with his glass.

At first, they just sat, taking in the starry night. A slight breeze rolled through. Carter sat back and exhaled.

"Thanks again for letting me come by."

"How's Zoe and Ethan?" Phoenix asked.

"She's resting. The baby is in the NICU. Only two pounds. She'll have to stay in the hospital for a while."

"Wow! Thank God she made it. I can't imagine..." Phoenix stopped speaking abruptly.

Carter knew why she stopped. Her situation wasn't the same, but he was sure it was just as stressful.

"About that," Carter said.

Phoenix swung her legs over the lounge chair she sat in and faced him. "I should have told you," she said. He remained quiet. "I realize that now. Back then, I was just angry, and distraught and scared."

Carter sat up and faced Phoenix. "You shouldn't have gone through that by yourself. That wasn't fair to you or me. My guilt won't let me be angry with you."

"Guilt?"

"I caused that stress that led you to your miscarriage. You lost our baby because of me." A lump lodged in Carter's throat. He swallowed hard and blinked harder. "Who else knows?"

"Just Savannah." Phoenix lay back again and stared at the sky.

"I left for a baby that wasn't mine and lost the one that was mine."

"I let you go without knowing you had a baby on the way."

Carter lay back now, too. Both kept their gazes toward the sky. Several beats passed before Carter sighed. "We screwed up, Phoenix."

"We did."

Nineteen

"You snuck out early," Phoenix said when she answered her cell phone. The morning sun poured through the window as she lay in the bed.

"I have early meetings and didn't want to wake you," Carter said.

"I'm exhausted." She yawned.

"I know. That's why I'm calling—to make sure you got up in time."

"Thanks," Phoenix said. "But I'm a big girl. I can handle a few late nights." Her smile radiated from deep inside.

"Okay, superwoman. See you later?"

"Why not?" Phoenix ended the call. She loved teasing Carter.

They were at it again. This was the third morning Carter woke up at Phoenix's house. Again, it was their secret.

Phoenix couldn't believe she was actually having a

rendezvous with her ex-fiancé. It would have to remain her salacious secret. Her mother would burst a blood vessel if she knew that she had been sleeping around with Carter. But the two of them fit together seamlessly. Phoenix had never felt so secure and complete with another man. Too bad it was temporary.

Happy thoughts followed Phoenix to the shower and work. She arrived early to take a phone interview. She wanted to get it over with before anyone else came into the office. It had been a while since she'd been on the job market. Phoenix was nervous about the interview but felt like she'd aced it. If they called her back, the next meeting would be in person.

Phoenix was glad that she was finally getting callbacks. The number of applications she'd submitted was too numerous to keep up with. She usually kept spreadsheets for things like this. Instead, she kept track of the job boards she used. Most were geared specifically to the technology industry. Phoenix also created a wish list of local tech companies to which she applied. A remote position would have been great also.

Indra knocked and stepped into her office.

"Morning!" she said.

"Morning!" Phoenix returned her greeting.

Indra sat on the edge of her desk. "We're making arrangements to fly the team out together the week after next. I was hoping we would know whether or not you were joining us."

Phoenix sat back. "I'll have an answer for you soon."

"Good. How's your dad?"

"Still struggling. He's still in the hospital. Another clot formed."

"Oh no! Sorry to hear that." Indra shook her head. "I know you have a lot going on. I don't mean to pressure you, but we need to know soon. We're hoping the extra time we gave to you to make the decision helps. If you can't join us when the team goes together, we're happy to fly you out later. But we can't wait too long."

"I understand. Just a little more time."

Indra cocked her head sideways. "I understand."

When Indra left, she thought about Carter. She hadn't mentioned anything about leaving since they'd been back from Fiji. A ball of angst formed in her stomach. She and Carter hadn't defined what they were doing. However, every moment they spent together slowly mended the damage they'd done in their past. She enjoyed his company. Being with him came with ease. She never intended to desire his company so much, among other things. Leaving would mean that this thing they had between them would have to be over. Phoenix wasn't sure she wanted that.

They had plans for dinner later. She decided to bring it up then. Thinking of him made her want to end her workday early. She giggled, thinking about the things they'd done to each other the night before. He'd fed her strawberries, kissing her between bites. The more they were together the more adventurous they became in bed and the more fun they had. Anticipating their date put a smile on her face that lasted the rest of the day.

Phoenix headed home to change before meeting up with Carter. The restaurant they chose was downtown, not far from either of their houses.

Phoenix's phone rang as she was getting into the shower. The display read Brent's name. She sent the call to voice mail. Brent had called two more times by the time she left her house. Instead of moving her car and worrying about finding parking on busy downtown streets, Phoenix took an Uber. Brent called again while she was in the car. She hesitated but answered.

"Yes, Brent?"

"Phoenix!" He sounded as if he'd been running.

"Everything okay?"

"Yes. I've been thinking. I want to apologize for my behavior. Let me come by so we can talk."

Phoenix drew in a sharp breath and released it in a rush. "That's not a good idea, Brent." She only answered the phone because he called back-to-back. There could have been an emergency.

"Phoenix…"

"I'm sorry, Brent. I truly wish you the best. I have to go. Good night." Phoenix ended the call and rubbed the back of her neck. How had she missed so many red flags with him? He was nothing like Carter. Brent called back but she refused to answer.

The car pulled up in front of the swanky restaurant. Phoenix exited and sauntered inside. She couldn't wait to see Carter. He greeted her with a kiss once she stepped in. They checked in and Carter placed his hand on the small of her back as the host led them to their reserved table. Carter pulled out her seat. Phoenix loved a man who treated a woman like a lady. That was another problem with Brent. He missed the mark on small things.

"You look amazing."

Phoenix had put special effort into her preparation. The black lace cocktail dress hugged her in all the right places. She'd even added false lashes, which made her feel sexy when she batted her eyes. Savannah would be proud. All this for Carter. Phoenix giggled.

"Thanks! You look quite handsome yourself." She wanted to say *delicious* but figured she'd save that for later. "So is this a date, Mr. Blackwell?"

"Phoenix."

She thought she heard her name. But it wasn't Carter who had called it.

"Phoenix!"

This time she knew she heard her name. Both Carter and she looked around. Brent was heading in her direction fast. Phoenix scrunched her face in frustration, then closed her eyes a brief moment to collect herself.

"Who is this, Phoenix? Is he why you won't talk to me?"

"Brent!" She spat his name. Carter stood. "Carter, no!" Phoenix was on her feet now. Every neck in the restaurant snapped in their direction. The host stepped toward their table. "How did you know I was here?"

Brent didn't answer. "Who are you?" Brent directed his question to Carter.

Carter's chest lifted. He took a step toward Brent. Phoenix maneuvered between the two men. Carter held her by the waist. Brent's eyes followed Carter's hand.

Brent turned to Phoenix. "Is this why you won't talk to me?"

"Brent. I told you it was over. You need to accept that."

"You heard the lady," Carter said calmly. "I'd advise you to leave now."

Brent shook his head. He took a step toward Phoenix. Carter gently moved her aside and stepped to Brent. "It's time for you to go." Carter was firm.

Brent didn't move. He looked from Carter to Phoenix. She hoped they wouldn't have to cause more of a scene than they already had.

"It's over, Brent. It's been over. You need to leave. Now!" Her nostrils flared. Heat flushed through her body.

Brent stood firm for another moment. All three held

their stances; none of them backed down. The host was now at their table. Brent huffed. Shook his head at Phoenix and walked away. She hoped she was seeing the last of him.

Once Brent was gone, Phoenix sat with her head in her trembling hands. She was furious.

"Want to get out of here?" Carter asked softly.

"Yes."

Carter placed money on the table. When Phoenix stood, he took her by the hand and led her outside. In silence they walked to Carter's car, got in and drove for a while. Phoenix didn't know where they were going and didn't bother asking. Carter pulled up by Canarsie Pier. He got out, rounded the car, opened Phoenix's door and held out his hand. She placed her hand in his. Carter led her to the railing where they could overlook the water.

"I come here when I need a moment of peace."

Phoenix smiled. "Thank you."

"No need." They remained silent for a while longer.

Phoenix started to feel better.

"Where'd you find that guy?" Carter said.

Surprised, Phoenix looked at him and found him laughing. She laughed, too.

Carter put his arms around her. She leaned onto his shoulder. Together they watched the moonlight ripple in the waves. There she was again. Safe in Carter's arms.

Before long they were swapping stories about their day. Carter updated her on Ethan, Zoe and the baby, and Phoenix updated him on her father's condition.

"So how long is your list of crazy exes?"

"Ha!" Phoenix swatted him playfully.

"I just need to know what I'm in for now that we're dating."

"Who said we're dating?" She narrowed her eyes at him and chuckled. Carter shrugged. They laughed but the comment tugged at Phoenix's heart. She couldn't seriously date Carter. Besides the fact that she may be leaving in a few weeks, her family would never accept him.

"Well, whatever it is that we're doing, I like it," Carter said. He kissed her. "I even brought strawberries."

"Your house or mine," Phoenix teased, knowing he was being naughty.

"Let's go." He took her hand, kissed it and walked her back to the car.

The attention he gave her made Phoenix giddy. They reached Carter's brownstone in record time. The door was barely closed before they started kissing. Peeling each other's clothes off, they left a trail from the entrance to the kitchen. Naked, they stood before his subzero refrigerator and pulled out a carton of strawberries. Carter washed the fruit and then laid Phoenix on her back across the large island. She flinched from the coolness of the countertop.

"I guess it's time for dessert." His voice was deep with desire. He took one of the strawberries, bit it and fed the rest to Phoenix. It wasn't long before he swept her naked body off the counter and carried her to his bed.

By the time they were done feasting on one another, their stomachs growled. Phoenix's stomach out-growled Carter's. Embarrassed, she covered her mouth with one hand and her belly with the other. Then she threw her head back and barked out a laugh.

Deciding to order in, they picked a comedy to watch and ate in bed. With her head against his muscular arm, she remembered what she meant to tell him. She watched him watch TV. Taking in his features as if she wanted to remember them precisely.

"Carter."

"What's up?" His eyes were on the television.

"I might be leaving soon."

Twenty

"Thanks, everyone, for your work tonight. This was good," Carter said to his colleagues at the Brooklyn branch office.

This was the last of several afternoon meetings his team had hosted in the past few days to quell their customers' growing anxiety about the volatile stock market. Carter hoped that would ease the angst of the few clients who called him every time a stock dipped in price. His wealthiest clients were used to the ups and downs. It was his newer and younger clients who required more hand-holding.

The staff left, but Carter went back to his office to send a few more emails. He rounded his large mahogany desk, trying to think of ways to connect with Roberts and secure his investment in the company. He still hadn't had the chance to meet with him since that day he missed their appointment. The longer it took, the more worried

Carter became about being able to convince Roberts to stick with him and Harris. The investment needed to launch; this company was massive. Having the right people involved was just as important as having the money they needed. He wanted to get this deal with Roberts solidified so he could deal with his father. Carter sat in his high-back executive chair and released a sigh. Bill wasn't going to be happy but he at least wanted to show his father that he had a solid plan.

It had always been hard to appease Bill. His brother Ethan worked so hard at gaining their dad's approval. For Carter, those efforts were too exhausting. It wasn't that he didn't think his father loved them. Bill seemed to believe that he needed to be extra hard on his boys. This was his way of preparing them for the world. The pressure to meet Bill's standards was often overwhelming. He had a vision for Blackwell Wealth Management that included all of his sons. Lincoln had already gone his own way and now Bill looked to Ethan and Carter to carry the mantle. What was he going to say when another son told him that Blackwell wasn't part of his future plans? Carter braced himself for his father's disappointment. Bill wasn't going to stop him from being his own man. He dreamed of building his own empire. That was something his father should be proud of. He couldn't stay under Bill's shadow forever.

Carter sat back in his chair, thinking of the best way to pin Roberts down. Instead of trying to catch him during the day, he thought of another way. Carter picked up his phone.

"Coop!" He called Harris by the name they called him in college.

"You heard from Roberts?"

"He hasn't gotten back to me yet. I've been trying to

schedule meetings during business hours. Why don't we just meet him for dinner? We can do Louie's," Carter suggested. Louie's was a posh steak house and popular spot in downtown Manhattan for major deals.

"Let me know what night works for you two and I'll make it happen on my end."

"You got it. I'll call you as soon as I hear back from him. Hopefully, it will be soon."

"Hope so!"

"All right. Check you later, bro." Carter ended the call.

With his business venture hanging in the balance and the most recent news bomb that Phoenix had dropped on him, Carter didn't have the capacity for much more stress.

Phoenix had a way with timing when it came to delivering news. Carter never expected that his one visit would turn into the two of them continuing to see one another on a consistent basis. After dealing with the past, he could now see a future for them. Hearing that she may be leaving the state made him realize how much he wanted a future with Phoenix. Would that consist of dating? An exclusive relationship? Carter wasn't seeing anyone besides her, nor was he interested. But now she may be moving across the country. Carter didn't want a long-distance relationship. He wanted Phoenix here with him. He hoped those other jobs she mentioned called. Then she wouldn't have to leave. It became clear to Carter that he wanted a second chance.

Carter called Phoenix to find out her plans for the evening. He told her to be ready for him around eight. The summer was approaching its end and the nights descended with a welcome breeze. Carter took that into consideration as he prepared for later. He made a few calls, pulled a few strings and his ideas were set in motion. That motivated him to shut down his laptop and leave the empty office.

Being in the Brooklyn office made it easy for him to get home quickly. Carter moved about efficiently. He showered and called the car service his company contracted for certain occasions. Instead of driving around New York City and searching for parking, he wanted to use that time to focus on Phoenix.

Carter moved like he was on a mission. Once his mind was made up, he didn't waste time. Within a half hour, Carter was well dressed in a black custom suit and white shirt. The car arrived right on time. The driver easily navigated the several turns it took to get from his brownstone to Phoenix's building. He still found it odd that she lived so close to him. Those sightings weren't his imagination. He was sure he'd seen Phoenix at local neighborhood businesses.

Carter stepped out of the car, tugged his jacket in place and headed to Phoenix's apartment. She opened after the second knock.

"Wow!" she said when she saw him. She finished placing an earring in her ear and looked down at her dress. "I need to change."

"You look beautiful." Carter laughed. "But go ahead if you must."

Phoenix went into the room and returned with a stunning black dress that draped off her shoulder. Carter, nearly speechless, could only stare in response. He shook his head. "And now you look stunning."

Phoenix winked. "That dress wasn't cutting it. So where are we going again?" Phoenix picked up her purse from the couch.

"I never said where we were going. However, you should probably bring a shawl."

"Oh. Okay." Phoenix went back into the room to grab a shawl. "So this is some sort of surprise."

"Maybe. As long as none of your ex-boyfriends show up."

"I doubt we have to worry about that."

Carter held out his elbow. Phoenix maneuvered hers around his.

The evening sky displayed a stunning show of orange, pink and yellow blends. It would be dark by the time they reached their destination in Manhattan. They filled each other in on their day during the ride.

Phoenix looked out the window when the car stopped. The driver opened the door and reached for her hand, helping her out of the car. Carter rounded the vehicle from the back, took Phoenix's hand in his and stepped into a contemporary structure squeezed between two traditional-looking buildings. They took the elevator to the penthouse floor and were greeted by a tall, well-structured gentleman in a tux.

"Mr. Blackwell! It's good to see you." The man gave a slight bow.

"Hey, Jeff. How are you this evening?"

"Well, sir." He turned his attention to Phoenix and nodded. "And you look stunning tonight, ma'am."

"Thank you." Phoenix smiled. She looked at Carter, pressed her lips together and lifted her brows. "Impressive," she teased.

Carter winked.

The gentleman led them onto the rooftop dining area with only a few couples seated sparsely to provide privacy. Their reserved table was the best in the house. It was a corner setting that offered an unhindered view overlooking Gramercy Park. He pulled out Phoenix's seat and then Carter's.

"Someone will be with you shortly to take your drink orders."

"Thanks, Jeff," Carter said.

"Well, this is special. What's the occasion?" Phoenix said once the host walked away.

"Another try at a real date."

Phoenix blushed. "Thanks."

"My boy, Carter!" Renowned Chef Chase Williamson declared as he reached their table. He flipped a towel across his shoulder.

"Chase!" Carter stood and hugged his friend and owner of the exclusive establishment.

"And this must be Ms. Phoenix." Chase took her hand and kissed the back of it.

Phoenix chuckled. "Hello. Just Phoenix is fine. I believe I've seen you on TV a time or two." She shook his hand.

"Tonight I prepared my special just for the two of you." Chase rubbed his hands together. "Coconut curry salmon over wild rice for you." He nodded in Carter's direction. Carter's mouth watered. "And for the lady, braised lobster over risotto topped with a creamy garlic and butter sauce and roasted Brussels sprouts on the side."

"I'm impressed." Phoenix smiled. "Thank you, Chase."

"Would you still like to start with the clams oreganata and grilled prawns?"

Carter glanced at Phoenix. She took that as her cue to answer on their behalf and nodded.

"Wonderful," Chase said cheerfully. "Bon appétit!"

"You're gaining points here, Carter. What's up?"

He smiled with Phoenix but his face quickly turned serious as he prepared his words.

"I want us to be together again."

Phoenix's water didn't make it to her mouth. She put the glass down. "Carter. Really?" Her brows furrowed.

"I know we've been through a lot. I take ownership of everything I brought to the table. I'm sorry. I want your forgiveness. I never meant to hurt you. I never thought we'd speak again." He took her hand across the table. "Being with you these past few weeks made me realize why I never committed to another woman. They were not you."

"Carter." Her voice was a whisper.

"I know now that I never stopped wanting you. But wanting you has stopped me from being with anyone else."

"Wow." Phoenix took that drink of water. She cleared her throat. "I may be leaving in a few weeks."

"Maybe you won't have to leave. You could start your own business."

"What about our families? My parents won't respond to this well."

"They will get over it," Carter said firmly. "It's what we want that matters. You know what I want. What do you want?"

"I... I don't know. I never thought we'd be here, either. I'm sorry for not telling you about the baby. But you hurt me so bad I couldn't think straight."

"And if you let me, I will make that up to you." Carter gazed directly into Phoenix's eyes.

Phoenix cast her eyes toward the ground.

"I know." Carter stood and rounded the table. He took her hand and led her to stand. With his index finger, Carter delicately lifted Phoenix's chin. "Give me this second chance." He kissed her lips. "Let me show you how much I care about you." He kissed her again. Phoenix lifted her chin and kissed him back. Carter licked his lips. She tasted sweet.

"And the move?" she asked.

"We will deal with that when and if it happens," Carter said. Now he had to find a way to get her to stay.

Twenty-One

"Phoenix!" Nadine's rasping breaths rushed through the phone. "Oh, my Lord. Phoenix!"

Phoenix snapped straight up in the bed. "Mom! What happened?" Her heart pounded in her chest. Carter sat up beside her. Concern was etched into his expression.

"Your father! Oh my goodness. Phoenix, he fell. We were going to the bathroom and he fell. He won't respond to me, Fi."

"Mom!" she shrieked. Phoenix threw the covers back, jumped out of bed and scampered around in search of her panties and leggings. Carter followed her lead, picking up his jeans from the floor. "Call the ambulance. I'm on my way. I'll call you when I'm on the road to find out where they're taking him." Phoenix heard her mother sniffle. "I'm coming, Ma! Daddy's going to be all right." Phoenix wanted to believe that. Tears spilled down her cheeks. "I'm coming." She tried to keep the fact that she was crying out of her voice.

"Please hurry, Fifi."

"I will, Ma." Phoenix pulled a college hoodie over her head, maneuvering with one hand at a time as she held the phone. "Wait! Did you call Savannah?"

"No. You're the first number I called."

"Hold on." Phoenix put her mother on hold and dialed Savannah. A quick glance at the clock and Phoenix realized it was after two in the morning. It took two attempts to get her sister on the phone.

"Hello." Savannah's voice was groggy. She cleared her throat.

"Savannah! It's Daddy."

"What! What's going on?" Savannah's voice was full now and laced with panic.

"Hold on." Phoenix merged the call and filled Savannah in on what little she knew. Savannah announced that she was on her way. "Savannah, let me know where they take him," Phoenix said, referring to the ambulance. "See you as soon as possible." As soon as she ended the call her tears started to flow. She prayed her dad would be okay.

Savannah lived on Long Island with their parents. Phoenix knew she would get there much sooner than her coming from Brooklyn. By the time she brushed her wild tresses up into a haphazard ponytail and left the bathroom, Carter was fully dressed, waiting on her.

"Where do we have to go?"

"We?"

"Yes. We. Don't argue with me. You're in no condition to drive. Now take off your shirt and put it on the right way before we leave."

Phoenix looked down and realized her sweatshirt was inside out. She chuckled through her tears but then burst into a full-on cry. She couldn't break down while she was on the phone with her mother. Carter wrapped his arms around her and held her trembling body. After several moments Phoenix pulled back and wiped her tears with the sleeve of her shirt.

Carter lifted the shirt over her head, righted it and put it back on, working with Phoenix as if she were a child, still needing help getting dressed.

"I'll drive." Carter kissed her forehead and led her by the hand.

Phoenix didn't protest. She could barely see through her tears. There was no way she could safely drive from Brooklyn to Long Island alone. She'd just tell Carter to stay in the car when they got to the hospital. She wasn't ready to explain to her family why she was with Carter Blackwell at nearly three in the morning.

Phoenix called her mother back when they got in the car. Nadine was inside the ambulance with her dad. She could hear the commands and commotion of the EMTs. Nadine whimpered as she tried to encourage her father.

"Hold on, honey. We're almost there." She told Phoenix which hospital to meet them at.

Next, Phoenix called Savannah. She and Jaxon were en route behind the ambulance. At that moment Phoenix felt like Brooklyn was too far away. It would be at least another twenty-five minutes before she got to them.

She ended the call, sat back in the passenger seat of Carter's SUV and let the tears roll down her cheeks. Carter took her hand in his, navigating the car as fast as he could with the other. Any other time she would have urged him to slow down. She needed to get to her family.

Finally, they arrived. Phoenix jumped out of the car and scurried through the entrance to the emergency room. She moved so fast she wasn't sure if she'd closed the door. She looked back. It was closed.

Phoenix's heart pounded in her chest. Her mouth dried. She begged God not to let anything happen to her father. Inside she inquired at the registration desk about her father. "Yes. Jones. Christopher. Yes."

The woman had soothing, sympathetic eyes. She directed Phoenix through a set of double doors manned by a burly security guard. He held the door for her. Phoenix scurried through the corridors, passed beds with patients lying asleep until she reached the number she was given.

"Ma!" she said when she thought she'd heard Nadine's voice.

"Phoenix!" Nadine poked her head outside the curtain. Her family was there but her father was not.

Nadine fell into her arms. Savannah wrapped her arms around Phoenix and Nadine. The three of them stayed that way for a while. Jaxon stood behind Savannah, rubbing her back.

When they released her, Phoenix said, "Where's Dad?"

"They're running tests," Nadine said.

Air swirled in Phoenix's chest like a rushing wind. She needed her father to pull through. She looked at her mother and held back tears. Nadine's weary eyes looked as if they hadn't seen sleep in days. Her usually flawless skin looked pale and dull.

"What did the doctors say?" Phoenix asked.

"It may be congestive heart failure. We'll know more when they're done running tests," Nadine said.

This could take all night. Phoenix felt her knees wobble. Savannah dropped her head into Jaxon's chest and cried.

"Okay." That was all Phoenix could say. She held Nadine's hand. She was at a loss for words. Again, she prayed for God to spare her father.

Jaxon left to find another chair. Phoenix sat when he returned. A moment later Phoenix heard her name. It was Carter. She froze. In that short amount of time, she'd forgotten he was with her and she hadn't told him to stay in the car. Now he was in the hospital at three in the morning. How would she explain that?

"That sounds like Carter," Jaxon said with his brows furrowed.

Nadine's face scrunched. "Why in the world would Carter be here?"

Phoenix said nothing. Nor did she move.

"Phoenix?" Carter's voice filtered through the curtains again. He was looking for her.

Jaxon stood and stepped outside the curtain. "Hey, man. What are you doing here?"

"I drove Phoenix."

"Oh…okay," Jaxon said.

Nadine looked confused, but then narrowed her eyes. Realization spread across Savannah's face. She raised her brow. Jaxon stepped back inside the curtain with Carter in tow. There was nothing to explain now. Carter's presence at almost three in the morning was explanation enough. She'd deal with her family later.

"Good evening, Ms. Jones." Carter nodded respectfully.

"Good evening, Carter," Nadine said but her eyes were on Phoenix's. "Thanks for bringing her to the hospital." She finally looked his way. Her tone was weary yet dry.

Nadine gave a tight nod in return and looked at Phoenix. She was certain that she was going to hear more from her mother later. He hugged Savannah and stood near Phoenix. Nadine watched all of their interactions.

The doctor stepped up and relieved her from the tension she was steeping in. He was a sturdy man with large shoulders, soothing blue eyes and a salt-and-pepper beard. He introduced himself as Phoenix tried to slow her heart rate with deep, cleansing breaths. The updates on her father's condition seemed bleak. They listened intently, crowding around the doctor as he spoke. Their father needed emergency surgery to open clogged arteries. It would take hours. He encouraged the family to go home, get some rest and return later.

"I'm not going anywhere," Nadine said. She was firm but polite. "You ladies go and I'll call you when he's out." She turned to the doctor. "Doctor, where can I wait?" Phoenix's heart broke for her mother. She wasn't going to leave her father's side.

"There's a family lounge. I can have someone show you there," Dr. Blake said.

"We're staying, too," Phoenix said, looking at her sister. Savannah nodded in agreement. Jaxon and Carter shared a knowing glance. They were staying, as well.

"So be it. I'll have someone show you there right away," Dr. Blake said. "She'll be here shortly."

Moments later a petite brown woman led them to the family lounge where they could wait for her father to get out of surgery.

In the hours that they waited, few words passed between them. They took turns napping on the uncomfortable chairs until the sun rose. Nadine paced, her arm folded across the other. Red lines wiggled through the whites of her eyes. Phoenix didn't think she'd gotten any sleep at all. Her mother went to the vending machine.

"Ms. Jones," Carter said. Phoenix's head snapped in their direction. "Jaxon and I will get you something to eat."

"I'm not actually hungry, Carter." Nadine's tone was

friendly. She seemed grateful. "I just need something to drink."

Carter stepped up to the machine and paid for five bottles of water and handed them out. Then he went to where Jaxon sat with Savannah's head resting in his lap. Phoenix stayed by her mother's side.

Moments later Jaxon and Carter announced that they were going out to get everyone something to eat. Taking orders they hurried off, leaving Phoenix, Savannah and their mom alone for the first time.

Nadine looked at Phoenix but she couldn't read her mother's expression. Phoenix stirred under her mother's gaze. "No need to talk about this now. Let's focus on your father."

Phoenix exhaled. Savannah's smile was sly. Phoenix was sure their mother didn't see it. Sometime after that Nadine went off to the ladies' room.

"What's up with that?" Savannah whispered when Nadine was completely out of earshot.

"What do you think?" Phoenix whispered back.

"I knew it." Savannah chuckled. "I'm kind of glad."

Phoenix shifted in her seat. "Why?"

"I just am. Did you tell him about the baby?"

Phoenix huffed. She gnawed on her lip a moment before saying, "Yes."

Savannah took Phoenix's hand in hers. "How did you feel?"

"Like a boulder has finally rolled off my shoulders." Phoenix looked down at Savannah's hand covering hers. "He called off the wedding because his ex, Taylor, was pregnant and she told him it was his baby. They dated just before we got back together and decided to get married. He found out after the baby was born that it wasn't his. He said he was only trying to do the right thing and be there for the baby. He said he didn't want to embarrass me with an illegitimate child months after we got married."

Savannah had covered her mouth with her other hand. "Oh my goodness! You plan on telling Ma?"

"For what? Carter and I are just...you know...enjoying ourselves. It's nothing permanent."

Savannah eyed her skeptically.

Phoenix thought about her job. Her father. Carter. She swallowed hard. It was too much to carry. She didn't want to talk anymore. But she did admit to herself that she was grateful for Carter's presence. Luckily, Nadine was on her way back toward them. Savannah's glance told Phoenix that she wasn't done with this conversation. The girls sat on either side of their mother and rested their heads on her shoulders.

Twenty-Two

"Roberts." Carter nodded and shook his hand. "Looking dapper as always." Carter noted his black designer suit, black shirt and fancy silk pocket square. Roberts's appearance was always polished with the slight essence of a well-dressed used car salesman.

"Evening, Blackwell."

"Cooper will be with us soon." The men had a thing about calling each other by their last names.

Carter nodded at the hostess in the posh steak house and she led them to their table.

The dim lighting and dark wood decor gave the decor a masculine feel. Empires were created over the dinner tables at Louie's Steak House. Carter planned to do just that, put the final piece in place to start his new technology empire. Carter and Harris agreed on the name Weller, combining the ends of their last names.

Snapping the napkin, Carter placed it in his lap.

"How's the family?" He started with small talk. Cooper arrived soon after.

"Pardon my tardiness, gentlemen," Cooper said as he sat.

The waiter quickly took their orders and they continued engaging in small talk until their dinner was served.

"Why the hesitancy, Roberts? Your feedback is important to me." Carter got right to the point.

"No investment from Blackwell. Your family is deeply entrenched in finance on the East Coast, real estate development in the Midwest and media on the West Coast. I found it odd that there was no backing from them."

"I see." Carter kept his cool. "Did you discuss this with my father?"

"Not directly. I realized he didn't know about it and that concerned me even more," Roberts said.

"I see." Carter leaned aside as the waiter placed their drink orders on the table. "I can assure you that Blackwell backing is in place." *Even if it wasn't coming directly from the head of Blackwell Wealth Management, Bill Blackwell.* "You could have asked me directly."

"At the same time, I'd been tapped for three other ventures and truthfully, the others were moving a bit faster. I had to make a decision to go with one of the others that were further along than yours. I doubt that any venture associated with Blackwell wouldn't be successful. But when the top Blackwell seemed oblivious to the opportunity, I questioned if it made sense to move forward. Speaking directly with you wouldn't have changed that."

"And your decision to meet with us today?" Harris asked.

"To let you know face-to-face."

"I can respect that." Carter glanced over at Cooper. He wanted to know how much Roberts had told his dad.

Bill hadn't given any indication that he'd known about his and Cooper's goals. "And my reason for wanting to meet with you today is for you to reconsider. I'd like to make you another offer for your investment."

Roberts lifted his chin as he slowly chewed the piece of filet mignon he'd just placed into his mouth. He nodded. That was Carter's cue to continue.

"I won't deny that having you among our pool of investors is impressionable. I know you're a staunch businessman. I also know that your investment in the other company won't hinder your ability to invest in Weller. We value not only your investment, but also your strategic mind and the strength of your network. And I know that we'll have better access to both with your investment. So this is a strategic ask and we're willing to sweeten the deal when it comes to your return. Also, Blackwell's support is guaranteed. I can send you numbers later if you're willing to hear more."

Carter placed a piece of steak into his mouth and waited for Roberts to respond. He buttered him up in preparation for the ask. His father had always taught him when to stop talking during deals. This was one of those moments. If Roberts was interested in hearing what else Carter had to say, he was sure his offer would urge Roberts to seal a deal with them.

Quiet filled the table except for the scraping of knives and forks and nearby chatter. The silence lasted long enough to begin to feel uncomfortable. Carter refused to speak.

"I'm listening," Roberts finally said.

Cooper flashed a quick smile.

"We're ready to up your stake in the company, fifteen percent, and would like for you to sit on the board. We're willing to pay a bit more for the added influence." Roberts smiled, confirming that Carter had stroked his ego. That was what he wanted. The promise of 15 percent guaranteed that Roberts would be the largest investor besides Carter and Cooper. "We need to know tonight."

Carter added that additional squeeze. He knew Roberts had the resources to meet the offer. He liked being schmoozed. He and Cooper had already agreed that their ceiling would be 15 percent with only one investor. They also had a feeling Roberts would be the one they'd ended up offering it to. Carter placed a tender piece of steak into his mouth and savored it.

Roberts put his fork down, wiped his hands on his napkin and shook his head. "You're strategic. Blackwell taught you well." He reached his hand over the table. Carter wiped his hand and shook Roberts's. Roberts did the same with Cooper. "We've got us a deal."

Carter felt like pumping his fist. Instead, he smiled. "I look forward to doing business with you." He raised his hand and got the waiter's attention. "Your best Cab, please." He turned to Roberts. "That is your favorite, right?"

"And you have a good memory," Roberts said and chuckled.

Carter's smug smile spread into laughter. The men enjoyed the rest of their meal. Their conversation turned to other subjects. They broached sports, travel, golf and the latest political scandals. Then Carter remembered something.

"Your other venture involves AI, correct?" Carter asked.

"Yes. Some great new technology, but I can't reveal anything about it," Roberts said, sitting back and sipping on his third glass of Cabernet.

"I have a friend in AI. She may be looking for a change and she's absolutely brilliant."

"They're in the process of building their team now. Have her give me a call."

Carter raised his glass. "Will do!"

Harris and Carter went over the changes to Roberts's deal on the phone once they were back in their cars. Carter felt like he could walk on clouds. This deal was back on and he was excited. The only thing he didn't look forward to was telling his father. He had to tread carefully now that Roberts revealed that he'd attempted to have a conversation with Bill. It concerned him that his father may have an idea about his venture without him being the one who told him.

He couldn't wait to get to Phoenix's house and fill her in. She'd be tired after spending another evening at her father's bedside. After spending that first full day with them during his surgery, Phoenix insisted he didn't have to come back. He knew why. Surely, Ms. Jones had thoroughly questioned his presence. Carter would never forget the shocked look on her and Savannah's faces when he walked into that emergency room. He caught Savannah's smirk. Jaxon looked surprised, too. Carter hadn't shared the fact that he was seeing Phoenix with him or his brothers. Until then, Phoenix was his secret. However, Carter wasn't interested in keeping her a secret anymore. These past few weeks confirmed for him that his heart still beat for her. She hadn't quite confirmed it, but he knew Phoenix felt the same way. But just like with his father, her parents wouldn't be elated about their reunion. He understood Phoenix's hesitancy but was convinced they could get over that.

Nadine had to know that if Carter was around at two

o'clock in the morning to drive Phoenix from Brooklyn to Long Island, it wasn't because Phoenix couldn't call an Uber. It had to be obvious to all of them that night that there was much more going on between Phoenix and him. That night also confirmed that she'd been keeping him a secret from her family the same way he had been keeping her a secret from his.

Carter was getting everything he wanted. The last thing he needed to work out was finding a way for Phoenix to stay. She would be more likely to stay in New York because of her father or a career opportunity and not just for him. He understood that.

Carter had been hoping that one of the positions she'd applied for would call her with an impressive offer. That hadn't happened yet. Hopefully, Roberts could deliver on that.

Carter pulled up to Phoenix's building and jogged inside. His excitement wouldn't allow him to walk. Positive energy surged through him. Phoenix opened the door. The heaviness of her mood was a sharp contrast to his elation.

"Hey." She leaned forward to kiss him. It had become customary between them. Both her greeting and her kiss were lackluster.

"Hey." Carter snaked his arms around her waist and kissed her again. "Dad okay?"

"He's out of ICU but not out of the woods. My poor mother won't leave his side. She's hardly eating."

"I'm sorry."

Phoenix breathed deep and exhaled with a groan and slipped from Carter's embrace.

"I have good news."

"I'd love to hear it." She plopped on the couch and pointed the remote at the television. The light from the

TV flickered throughout the room. She put it on mute. "What happened?"

"Roberts is back in. The deal is still on."

"That's wonderful!" Phoenix managed to muster a bit of excitement for her response. "Have you told your father?"

"This week. I wanted to make sure things were ready to move before bringing it up. Have you heard anything back from the other companies?"

Phoenix pressed her lips together and then huffed. "Nothing since that last callback for a chief technology officer. They said they wanted to conduct an interview but I haven't heard anything back."

Phoenix folded her legs under herself on the couch and leaned on her hand. She looked like she was ready to lose hope.

"What's Indra saying about your move?"

"I bought some time when I told them about my dad. If nothing else comes through, I'll be leaving the middle of next month. They're already working on my accommodations. I'm just hoping my dad is better by then."

Carter sat facing her on the couch. "Just stay."

Phoenix touched his face. "Carter. I can't. I really love my job. California isn't my first choice, but it can't be that bad."

"I get it," Carter said. And he did. Just like him, Phoenix's decisions had to be on her own terms. At that moment he decided not to tell her about the opportunity with the company Roberts was investing in. Instead, he'd find out who was doing their recruitment and he'd make sure they had an eye on Phoenix.

"You seem exhausted. I'll come back by tomorrow after you get in from visiting your father." Carter kissed her lips and stood.

Phoenix caught him by the arm. “No! Don’t leave.” Her voice was a mix of fatigue and seduction.

Carter smiled deep on the inside. He lifted her into his arms. She loved when he did that. Carter carried her to the bedroom and laid her down. He removed his shirt and pants, climbed into bed and held her. She held him back until they fell asleep together.

Twenty-Three

"Hey, Mom!" Phoenix whispered as she eased out of bed, trying not to wake Carter.

"You're just getting up? No wonder you didn't answer my calls this morning. I was trying to get you to come and have breakfast with me. I want to talk to you."

Phoenix looked at the clock as she tiptoed out of the room. "We could do lunch. What would you like to talk about?" She grabbed a bottled water from the refrigerator and sat on a stool near the breakfast nook.

"Why are you whispering? Is Carter there? Phoenix." Nadine said her name like she pitied her. "What are you doing with him?"

"Mom."

"Don't *Mom* me! You don't remember how much pain, and money and embarrassment he caused you?"

"Yes, Mom. I do."

"What would our family say—our friends, if they saw

you taking up time with him after all he had done? How would that make us look?"

"Us?" Phoenix scrunched her face.

"Yes. Us. You didn't go through all that embarrassment by yourself. That was one of the most humiliating events of my entire life!" Nadine was yelling.

"I don't want to talk about this." Phoenix threw her hand up.

"What happened to that other guy you were dating? What's his name, Bob?"

"Brent and he was worse than Carter could ever be."

"Oh, please. Phoenix. I don't get it."

"I know, Mom. And that's okay."

"Okay!" Nadine screeched. "You're not serious about being with him, are you? I would never accept him."

She saw Carter walk from her bedroom to the bathroom. If Nadine knew that they spent almost every night together at her house or his, she'd have a fit.

"I'm sorry, Ma. I have to go." She paused a moment. "I love you." Phoenix ended the call with her mother still yelling her name.

Phoenix expected this. This was why she kept this thing between her and Carter to herself. She even tried to keep Carter at a distance in her heart. It didn't work. She was falling for Carter all over again. Phoenix wanted to be with him more every day. Carter was everything all the men she dated after him were not. She never realized how much she'd missed him. But being with him would create friction between her and her mother. Possibly her entire family. How could she choose between the man she was falling in love with and her own family?

Carter came from the bathroom and sat on the stool next to her. "Feeling better?"

"A little."

"Got plans for the day?"

"A few errands. Going to see my dad. I need to start packing and my mom just asked me to lunch."

"Oh! The packing."

"Don't start, Carter."

He held his hands up in surrender. "I'm not saying anything. I'm heading to Long Island, too. The family is getting together for brunch and then we're going over to see the baby at the hospital."

"How are they?"

"Much better. Zoe's been home for a couple of days now and doing well. The baby is still in the hospital but getting stronger every day. She's a feisty one. The doctors said she'll be able to come home in a few weeks."

"Oh, that's such great news!"

"Shower?" Carter asked.

"Sure." Phoenix slid off the stool and let Carter lead her. "Wait! Carry me."

Carter chuckled and swept her off her feet.

She loved having him around and wanted to get as much time with him as possible until she left. Phoenix wasn't sure what it would be like when she left, but she knew she was going to miss him terribly. It would be like having her heartbroken all over again. She didn't voice how she felt, but was sure he already knew.

As they hit the bathroom door, Phoenix heard her doorbell. Sliding out of Carter's arms, she wondered who it could have been. The series of knocks answered her question. No one rang and knocked like that besides Savannah. That was their signal.

"It's Savannah!" She ushered Carter into the bathroom. "Enjoy the shower."

"All right." Carter kissed her, gathered his belongings and headed to the shower.

The ringing and banging continued. "Okay. Okay. I'm coming."

Phoenix opened the door and Savannah dashed in like a rushing wind.

"What took you so long?" Savannah's energy was always on ten. She craned her ear toward the running water. "Oh! You were just about to take a shower? Good. I came to take you to lunch so we can talk."

Phoenix rolled her eyes. "Like Mom wanted to talk this morning."

"She called, huh? She's been on a rampage since Carter showed up at the hospital, asking me all kinds of questions and getting mad when I told her I didn't know the answers. She told me I was trying to cover for you."

"Ugh! Well, she let me know exactly how she felt a little while ago."

"Save it for lunch. Go get in the shower."

"Um." Phoenix averted her eyes.

"Um. What?"

Phoenix tilted her head in the direction of the bathroom.

"Oh!" Savannah said. "He's here. Is that why Mom freaked out? Hey, Carter!" she yelled. "I'll be out on the balcony." Instead, Savannah walked in the opposite direction toward the kitchen. "After I make me a cup of coffee." She opened the refrigerator. "You got French vanilla creamer? Never mind, I'll find it."

Phoenix headed for the bathroom, shaking her head. "In the refrigerator door."

"Enjoy!" Savannah said and snickered.

Phoenix and Carter dressed quickly. He stopped to say hello to Savannah on his way out.

"Hey, Carter." Savannah's slick smile made Phoenix shake her head. Carter laughed.

"Hi, Savannah. How's the newlywed life treating you?"

"I love it. How's the reunited life going for you?"

"Savannah." Phoenix cocked her head to the side.

She snickered again. "I'm just teasing. I don't think it's bad. Things are usually better the second time around. At the end of the day, you have to do what makes you happy even if it makes others unhappy."

Carter and Phoenix looked at each other.

"See you later?" Phoenix dismissed Carter.

"Yeah. Call me when you get back to Brooklyn." They kissed.

Savannah cleared her throat. "I'm still here but don't mind me. Ha!"

Carter waved at Savannah before walking out. "Later, cousin."

"You're a mess," Phoenix said.

"And you were never fooling anyone. I knew you still held a torch for that man. You were just angry. Heck! I was angry, too. He made a jilted bride out of my sister, but I also knew that you never stopped loving him."

"That's not true." The words rushed past Phoenix's lips.

Savannah's expression turned serious. "I've always been able to see what you couldn't, sis. And what you refused to see. Despite your past you're letting him into a place you haven't allowed a man into for five years." Savannah tapped the center of Phoenix's chest.

Phoenix didn't respond. She couldn't. Savannah was right. That was why Phoenix needed to go ahead and take the job in California. If she stayed, she'd be in Carter's arms every night and she couldn't have Carter and her family. Her mother made that clear.

Twenty-Four

Carter took a few days off to handle business for Weller. Their agreement with Roberts had been signed and the money transferred. Harris took the lead on hiring and Carter worked on getting their offices set up. They were still a few weeks away from an official launch but Carter's window of opportunity to speak with his father was closing. He wanted to give Blackwell at least a month's notice.

On his first day back in the office, the executive team was meeting at the headquarters for monthly management meetings. Carter decided to have the conversation with his father after the meeting was over.

He called Roberts while he waited for the meeting to start.

"Morning. I was checking in about the opportunity with that AI company we spoke about," Carter said.

"Oh yes. You were going to send me your friend's information."

"Yes. However, I'd rather orchestrate an introduction. I don't want her to know that I'm trying to help her."

"I see," Roberts said. "How about I introduce the two of you by email and you can take it from there."

"That sounds like a plan. Thanks!"

"Not a problem."

When Roberts sent the email, Carter planned to share Phoenix's credentials with him and if they wanted to reach out to her, they could. He was sure that once they saw her résumé, they'd want her on their team. He'd let her know that he'd had a small hand in getting her the opportunity if something came of it. His goal was to help Phoenix secure a position in New York so she wouldn't have to leave.

Carter believed he and Phoenix could make it as a couple. Though he kept their situation to himself, he wasn't concerned about what their families had to say. All that mattered was that he was falling in love with Phoenix again. He wanted to spend his life making up for every mistake he'd made with her. He was confident Phoenix cared for him as much as he cared for her but if she moved across the country that would hinder their chances of building a life together.

One by one the rest of the Blackwell management team strolled in, chatting, drinking coffee and eating the pastries the office manager had set up for them in the conference room. Ethan walked in and everyone applauded. It was his first management meeting after his return back to work. He'd been out since Zoe's hospitalization.

"Thanks, guys." He put his head down, lifted it back up and smiled.

Dillon, the regional director for the Westchester

branches hugged him. “Congrats, man! We’ve been rooting for you and Zoe.”

“I appreciate it.”

“Tell Zoe we miss her,” one of the branch managers said.

“Good morning.” Bill stepped in with his booming voice and commanding presence. Despite his stature, he still exuded warmth.

“Good morning, Bill!” several people said.

Ethan and Carter greeted their dad.

“Good to see you back, son,” Bill said to Ethan.

“It feels good to be back, old man,” Ethan said.

Bill chuckled.

“Hey, Dad. You busy after the meeting? I want to talk to you about something,” Carter said.

“I always have time for you, son.”

“Thanks, old man,” Carter said.

Bill cleared his throat, quieting the room. “It’s great to see you all. I’ll start by saying how glad I am to see my son Ethan return. We’ve missed both you and Zoe here and continue to wish you the best. We must acknowledge and applaud Bella for her amazing work, stepping in for Zoe at the branch. Blackwell continues to grow. Please grab something to eat or drink and take your seats. We’ve got a full agenda today and I’d like to get started right away.”

The team did as Bill instructed. They got right down to business reporting on the numbers at each branch, company objectives and breaking them down by region and branch.

“Despite market fluctuations, we’ve been able to calm our clients’ fears and still grow our customer base across the entire region. Our information sessions were instrumental in allowing us to stay connected to our clients and led to a significant number of referrals," Carter reported.

Each region gave their reports and before Carter knew it, they were approaching lunchtime. He thought about the conversation he was about to have with his father and rubbed the back of his neck. Once all the reports had been presented, the team applauded, celebrating another successful month in spite of trying economic times.

"Before we close out, I want to make a special announcement." Everyone turned their attention toward Bill. "As some of you may know, I will be sixty years young very soon." He laughed. "And as I approach that milestone, I'm considering my next phase in life. I've made it known that it's been my dream to hand my company over to my sons Ethan and Carter. They have certainly proven themselves capable and I look forward to beginning the process of passing the mantle to these fine gentlemen."

A few began applauding until the entire room clapped and cheered for Ethan and Carter.

"I also want the rest of our team to know we've got our eyes on you, too," Bill continued. "I'm confident that some of you, like Bella, have what it takes to step into bigger roles. We're ready to provide opportunities for professional development and mentorship to help prepare all of you for your next step whether it be with Blackwell or not. I want all of you to be successful."

Everyone in the room seemed to be excited about Bill's announcement except Carter. Without warning, his father had just announced handing over the reins of the company to him and Ethan on the same day Carter planned to hand in his resignation.

The meeting came to a close. Saying their goodbyes,

everyone began to clear out. As VP, Ethan now had his offices officially at the headquarters.

"What's my niece up to?" Carter asked Ethan.

"Getting stronger every day. She's developed some set of lungs. I'll be honest. That crying is music to my ears. The doctor said yesterday that we might be able to bring her home sooner."

"What did you expect? She's a Blackwell."

"Ha!" Ethan nodded. "You're right."

"Hey." Bill walked up to them. "You men ready to run Blackwell?"

"As long as we don't have to share offices," Ethan teased.

The brothers looked at each other and laughed. "It was hard enough sharing a room with you as a kid," Carter added.

"Ha!" Bill threw his head back and let out a hardy laugh. He put a hand on each of their shoulders. "You have no idea how proud I am of you young men. I dreamed of the day I would get to hand over the company. The legacy begins." Bill beamed. "Oh. Carter. You wanted to talk to me, right?"

Carter felt his smile fade. "Uh. It was nothing big. I need to get back. I planned to stop by the Queens office today." Carter looked at his watch. "Catch you later, Ethan." The brothers hugged. "I'll see you this weekend, Dad."

Carter would tell his father. It just wasn't going to be today while Bill's chest was puffed with pride.

Twenty-Five

"Taking these?" Savannah held up a pair of black stiletto booties. "You may have a hot date with a cute technology geek!"

Phoenix laughed. "Silly! We're not your everyday geeks." Phoenix tilted her head. "Well, maybe. Throw them in the box."

"I certainly hope you find a nice man. I'm happy you're getting away from that Blackwell boy," Nadine said.

"Mom. Please don't start."

Nadine huffed and waved away Phoenix's reprimand.

"Ugh!" Savannah picked up a box and carried it from the bedroom to the living room and placed it in the designated corner with the others. "When are the movers coming?"

"Friday."

Nadine stopped placing the clothes from the pile on

the bed into the suitcase in front of her and sat still. After a moment she said, “What day do you leave again?”

“Next Monday,” Phoenix said.

“Oh!” Nadine placed her hand on her heart. “I’m going to miss you so much.”

Phoenix went to her mother and hugged her. “I’m going to miss you, too, Mom. Thanks for coming to help me pack.”

“Your dad is going to miss you, too. You girls never strayed too far from us,” Nadine said in a quiet voice. Her eyes filled with tears. She took a breath, shook her head and breathed deep.

“Yeah.” Phoenix sat next to Nadine and laid her head on her shoulder. “I know.” Nadine patted Phoenix’s hand. They remained quiet for several moments. “I’m so glad he’s finally home. I didn’t want to leave while he was still in the hospital.”

“You know he tried to come and help today.” Nadine tsked and shook her head.

“That’s Dad,” Phoenix said. Both chuckled.

“Hey! You two back here getting emotional while I do all the work?” Savannah parked her hands on her hips.

Phoenix cut her eyes toward the ceiling. Savannah raced to where they sat on the bed and wrapped her arms around both of them and yelled, “Group hug!” making all three of them laugh.

“Let’s call it a day. I’m hungry,” Phoenix said.

“Me, too!” Nadine said. “Let’s order something. I need to get back to Chris. I don’t like to leave him alone for too long.”

“I’ll grab the menus.” Savannah hopped to the kitchen.

Nadine chose sushi and the girls followed suit. They continued chatting over their meals on the balcony before Savannah and Nadine headed home.

After saying goodbye, Phoenix grabbed a bottle of wine and a glass, and headed back to the balcony. It was a beautiful night. Stars sparkled brightly against a velvety black sky. A slight breeze caressed her skin. The sounds of Brooklyn mumbled in the distance, cars, horns, the whistle of the air. They all blended into a soft symphony. She was on a high enough floor so the city's natural soundtrack wouldn't be a huge distraction.

Phoenix hadn't been alone on a Saturday night in weeks. If she wasn't at Carter's house, then he was at hers. But not tonight. Carter was with his family. She wondered what it would have been like to hang at his family's house with him like they used to. Would they even welcome her?

Until Savannah's wedding, she'd been cool and distant with the Blackwells. She knew for sure that her parents wouldn't welcome him with warmth and open arms. She'd known people whose boyfriends or girlfriends didn't get along with their family. It was a burden that she didn't want to carry. Despite that, she enjoyed being in Carter's presence and wished things between him and her parents could be different.

She thought back to their time together in Fiji. For a few days, they had been the old Carter and Phoenix, adventurous and fun. There was nothing they wouldn't try together. He got her. No other man after Carter ever did.

Nadine was right. What would it look like if they actually got back together? Phoenix was never one to care much for what people had to say. That was more Nadine and Savannah, but surely there would be lots of buzz. She could just imagine walking into events or showing up for holidays on Carter's arm. Phoenix chuckled out loud. She could see it now, wide eyes and open mouths on shocked faces. Then the whispers would start. Those bold enough would come directly to them and ask silly, obvious questions. "Are you two together?"

Who mattered? Them or her? If Carter was what her heart wanted, why should she care what others had to say? Phoenix groaned. That idea was easier said than lived. Moving allowed her to leave it all behind. Silicon Valley would give her a fresh start. She'd come back for holidays, long weekends and vacations. Maybe she could come back sometime and just let Carter know that she was in town. They could spend the weekend holed up in her apartment without interruption. Phoenix laughed aloud. That didn't make any sense. Who would she be hiding from? Who was she lying to?

Herself.

Phoenix closed her eyes. She breathed deep and groaned. Who was she fooling? She'd fallen in love with Carter Blackwell all over again. But what could she do about it? In less than ten days, she would be on a plane to her new life in California. Even if she stayed, life with Carter would be too complicated to enjoy openly. She hated that she cared so much. Nadine had made herself clear. She was close with her mother and would hate to ruin their relationship. But Phoenix was a grown woman and had never let Nadine dictate her life. Why would she do so now?

Phoenix stood and walked to the corner of her balcony. She could hear the neighbor's music. Her favorite, R & B from the nineties. She'd grown up with her parents telling her that it was among the best music. Love songs today weren't the same as the ones her parents listened to. She felt the love and the pain in the music from the seventies, eighties and nineties. It penetrated their souls then. Hers, too.

Phoenix leaned against the railing, swaying to the

rhythm. The song changed; she kept listening. She heard the words "If you think you're lonely now, wait until to-night." Phoenix held up her glass and laughed. She was lonely. As long as she'd been living alone, she never felt lonely, until tonight. Carter's absence left a void.

Her cell phone rang. She wanted it to be Carter. She hadn't called him because she didn't want to bother him when he was with his family. Phoenix walked back to the wicker table next to the chair she'd been sitting in and picked up her phone. It was Carter. Her grin could not be contained.

"Hey, you."

"What are you doing?" Carter asked. The sultry sound of his voice made her yearn for his presence. She was going to miss him so much when she left.

"Relaxing on my balcony."

"I wish I were there with you."

"How's your dad's birthday shindig going?" Phoenix asked. She could hear the celebration in the background.

"Oh. It's great! He's having the best time. My mother and sister really outdid themselves. The venue is on the water. The view is amazing, the food was delicious and he's surrounded by his family and friends. What more could he ask for?"

"That's great!" She forced a smile. Mr. Blackwell's party sounded wonderful. The idea of being surrounded by family and friends made her sad. Besides coworkers, she'd have no one in California.

"I guess you'll be getting home pretty late."

"Yeah." There was a pause. "Did you do more pack-ing?"

"Yes. My mom and Savannah came and helped me today."

"That's cool.

"I wish you didn't have to go."

"Carter!" she sang, admonishing him.

"I know. I'm not supposed to keep saying that but it's true. I'm going to need to spend as much time as I can with you before you get on that plane. I told you I could come and help you get settled," Carter said.

"And I told you that I'd be fine." Phoenix needed a clean break. The lingering would only torture her. Trying to get through this one night was bad enough. Phoenix wasn't going to tease herself with pop-up visits. The secrecy had already been more than she could stand. She wanted all or nothing with Carter. And she had no choice but to choose nothing.

"Let's make sure this last week together is memorable," Carter said.

"I'd like that," Phoenix said and blushed.

"I guess I should get back to the party," Carter said.

"Yeah. Enjoy." Under different circumstances, she would have told him to tell his siblings she'd said hi.

"See you tomorrow?" Carter said.

"Yes."

"Okay. Good night," he said. Yet, no one ended the call.

Phoenix lay back on the lounge chair with the phone to her ear. After a while she said, "Call me on your way home if you want to talk."

"I will," Carter said. Still no one hung up. They listened to one another breathe. Finally, Carter said, "I love you."

Phoenix squeezed her eyes shut, opened them and ended the call.

Twenty-Six

Carter thought about how much he'd enjoyed being immersed in family for his father's birthday weekend as he drove through his parents' neighborhood. It was a far cry from the dense streets of Brooklyn and his brownstone that was beautiful and historical, but narrow and tight. He drove through two-laned streets with sprawling homes set far back from the hilly road, with lush trees that gave natural privacy. This was the last of the planned festivities for his father's milestone birthday.

As much as he enjoyed spending so much time with his family, he couldn't wait to get back to Phoenix. Carter missed her presence. He thought about asking her to come with him but he knew she wouldn't. Waking up alone felt odd. He thought about her all through the day, every day. With only a week left, he remained hopeful that something would come through for her and she wouldn't have to leave. The thought of her packing troubled him.

The words he'd said to her last night on the phone played in his head over and over again. He'd felt it but never voiced it. Yet, he'd parted his lips and the words "I love you" escaped his heart easily and naturally. He hadn't given it any thought and only realized what he had said after he'd said it.

Carter didn't want to push Phoenix. They'd been through enough. If Phoenix wished to stay, or love him, he wanted her to come to those conclusions on her own. His call to Roberts was to help her find opportunities she'd already been seeking. If it worked out, then great. If it didn't, he'd have to deal with her absence. Maybe he'd find love again though he knew it would never be like it was with Phoenix. It was as if their past hardships made their bond even better this time.

Carter maneuvered up the private drive and around to the side of his parents' massive home. Several cars were already in the driveway. Unlike the black-tie event of the night before, today's brunch was casual and held at their home with a color scheme of silver and Bill's favorite, green.

Carter needed to tell his father about Weller before he left their home tonight. The office wasn't the right place and over the phone would be unacceptable. Carter would wait until all the guests, which were mostly family, had gone for the evening. He could tell both his mother and father together.

Entering through the garage door, Carter greeted his mother first.

"Hey, sweetie," Lydia said.

"Hey, Mom." He pulled her into a bear hug and lifted her off her feet.

"Put me down, boy," she said, smiling. She popped

him in the arm. "Your dad is outside with Eloise and his brothers."

All of Bill's brothers and his only sister flew to celebrate with him. Originating from South Carolina, the Blackwell clan was bred in New York and spread across the country. They had empires in different industries, such as media, real estate development, finance and hospitality. The family was massive and when they got together, the gatherings were massive. Some of them were heading back later that evening. So Carter decided to wait until the majority of them left. In the meantime, he'd enjoy the company of his many cousins.

Carter greeted his father, who was on the upper deck enjoying cigars with his brothers, Tommy, Ben and Melvin. Eloise, his stylish only sister, was on the lower deck with the ladies. Aunt Eloise was a grand Southern belle even though she was raised in Queens until she left for college in Atlanta where she met her husband.

"Hey, Carter." He greeted his uncles one by one with hugs and fist bumps. They teased him about being a bachelor.

"Are you still allergic to commitment?" his uncle Tommy asked. The rest snickered.

"Come back to LA with me," Uncle Ben teased. "There's plenty of beautiful women to choose from there. You see Tyson finally settled down with Kendall. She sings like a beautiful bird. You know she's got another movie coming out."

"I saw that. I'll be the first one at the theater. In fact, where's Kendall and Tyson? I want tickets to the premiere!"

The men laughed. Carter moved on to greet his other family members. Several areas of the house both inside and out were filled with groups of cousins from both his mother's and father's sides.

Carter caught up with his brothers and a few of his male cousins in the guesthouse. The female cousins hung out with the wives and girlfriends. For the next few hours they ate heartily, talked trash and told embarrassing stories from their childhood. Several times Carter wondered what it would have been like had he and Phoenix married. They would have been among the married cousins swapping stories about the kids and married life. Phoenix would have been there with him.

"Carter!" Lincoln said his name.

"What's up?" he answered.

"Dude! I called you three times. What's on your mind?"

"Ah! Work." Carter said the first thing he could think of. Between the conversation he had to have with his father and thoughts of Phoenix constantly creeping up, Carter couldn't help zoning out. "Thinking about some stuff I have coming up this week."

"No thinking about work!" one of his cousins said. "Not today."

"You're right." They pulled Carter back into the conversation.

As family members began to say their goodbyes, Carter went through the motions but his mind was on "the talk." He sat at the island and rubbed his hands across the smooth marble countertop and then down the legs of his pants. Finding something to do with his hands had become a challenge. Bill walked in through the double doors leading from the backyard. Carter stood.

"Heading home now, son?" Bill asked.

"Yeah. Can I have a word with you for a moment before I go?"

"Sure." Bill's brow furrowed. "Is everything all right?"

"Yeah. Let's talk in your study."

Bill headed in that direction. Carter followed and closed the door behind them.

"Do I need a drink?"

"Well..."

"What is it, Carter?"

Carter took a breath. "I'm leaving Blackwell."

His father's expression fell. A combination of anger and disappointment flashed across his hooded eyes.

"Carter!"

"I realize you're getting ready to retire. I appreciate all that you've taught me, but I want to build my own empire."

Bill's jaw squared; the muscles in his face seemed more rigid. He sat back in his executive chair, hard. With his hand on his chin, he wore a pensive gaze. He didn't look in Carter's direction. He didn't speak.

Carter became uncomfortable in the thickening silence.

"I built this company for you. For my children. To leave a legacy. I want to leave it in the hands of my heirs."

"I'm sorry, Dad. I want the same thing, but my own."

"So your kids can disappoint you and toss everything you built back in your face? First Lincoln. Now you! Ethan will have to carry this company on his own shoulders!" Bill stood and groaned. His comment stung Carter. He knew he would be upset, but that cut. "When do you plan on leaving?"

"Thirty days."

"What are you going to do?"

"Harris and I have been working on a venture. We finally have all of our investors in place. The name is Weller, a technology firm."

"Those are expensive and risky investments."

"You've taught us to never run from risk."

Bill narrowed his eyes at Carter.

"Dad. I need to do this. If it doesn't work, hopefully, you'll welcome me back. But I have to give it a try. My heart, money and all of my resources are in this thing."

"Why are you just telling me?"

"Because I knew how you'd react."

Bill sat back. He rubbed his chin for a long time. Emboldened, Carter stood firmly in the tension that threatened to suck the oxygen from the room. He couldn't wait any longer. It wouldn't be fair to him or his father.

"I'll need you to figure out your replacement. We will announce your resignation tomorrow." Bill stood and walked out of the room.

Carter ran his hand across his forehead. The hard part was over. He'd had the conversation with his father. He got his business. Now he needed to get his woman.

Twenty-Seven

The first email in Phoenix's inbox was from a recruiter. They wanted to speak with her about a position at a new company that was launching in New York. She tried not to get too excited. After closing her office door, she returned to her chair and dialed the number in the signature line. Normally she would have just responded by email, but she was anxious so she took a chance by calling.

"Leah Dresner." The woman's voice was full of life for a Monday morning.

"Hello, Ms. Dresner. This is Phoenix Jones, calling regarding your email about an opportunity with a technology company launching in New York."

"Yes! Ms. Jones. I'm so glad you called. We came across your information. Your credentials seem impressive. I wanted to speak with you regarding a position our client is seeking to fill. I can give you some insight now and you can let me know if you're interested in having me set up an interview."

"Sure. I'd love to hear about it."

Phoenix listened to Leah describe the company and the opportunity. The more she spoke, the more Phoenix became excited. This start-up must have had an incredible amount of financial backing. And they seemed to know quite a bit about her accomplishments. The offer was more impressive than what her current boss wanted to give her. The idea of being on the ground floor of such an amazing opportunity in tech enticed her even more.

"Does that sound like something you'd be interested in?"

"Absolutely!"

"Wonderful. Would you be available to come in for an interview next week, Wednesday?"

Leah had just put a pin in her excitement bubble. "Unfortunately, I will be leaving town on Monday. Is it possible to get an earlier interview?"

"I'm not sure, but I'll check. Is this a good number to call you back on?"

"Yes. It's my cell."

"Okay. Great. I'll see what we can do and get back to you ASAP!"

"Thanks. I look forward to speaking to you."

Phoenix ended the call and squealed. Hopefully, this one would work out. She pulled up the website the recruiter had given her to find out more about the company. She also found a few articles touting their launch. They were brand-new but backed by some major players. Projections about how they would fare were very favorable. Phoenix sat back and thought for a moment. She hadn't applied for a position with them. How had this recruiter found her? She assumed it was through one of the job boards.

The first call she made was to Carter.

"Good morning, beautiful. I missed you last night."

"I missed you, too. I have good news. Well, it's still too early to tell but I'm excited about it." Phoenix told Carter about the job.

"That's great! So if this comes through, you won't have to leave."

"If! And that's a big *if.* I may not be able to get an interview before I leave."

"How about I come take you out to lunch to celebrate?"

"I've got meetings all day. I'm going to be glued to this desk. How about dinner?"

"I'll take it. Good luck. I'll keep my fingers crossed for you."

"Great!"

That call put Phoenix in a great mood. She opened her door again. There were only a few people left at the office. Those who were not moving and one who was leaving next week like she was. Indra and Dean had been in California for the past two weeks.

Phoenix headed back to her desk and prepared for back-to-back meetings. She sailed through the day on her excitement. Her mood changed when she realized it was after two in the afternoon and she hadn't heard back from Leah Dresner. She thought about calling her back, and changed her mind. Phoenix handled some work before her next meeting. As she was about to leave her office and meet her coworkers in the conference room, her phone rang. It was Leah.

"Phoenix Jones."

"Ms. Jones. Leah Dresner. How are you?"

"I'm well. And you?"

"I'm well, thanks. We were able to get an interview

moved up but the window is tight. Would you be available to meet tomorrow morning?"

"I would have to move some stuff around but I could definitely make it happen."

"Great! How's nine thirty?"

"Perfect. Where?"

Leah gave her the address. The office was right in downtown Brooklyn, not far from Phoenix's current job. They finalized the details. When the call was over, Phoenix jumped up and danced around her desk. She hoped this worked out. The closer she got to her move date, the more she realized she wasn't interested in leaving New York. The only relief it would have provided was leaving Carter behind so she wouldn't have to deal with how complicated life had become. She wanted him but didn't like the burden that came with being with him because of her family. If she stayed, she'd have to deal with that somehow.

Phoenix remembered Carter's words the other night when she was on the phone. He'd said he loved her. She already knew that. She knew Carter. She also knew that she loved him, too. If it didn't come up she didn't have to face it. But Carter brought it up and made her acknowledge her own feelings.

Phoenix shook away those thoughts. She didn't want to deal with that now. If this job didn't come through, she was back to her original plan of leaving. Whether she left or stayed, it wouldn't make life easier. Leaving Carter behind would be an adjustment. If she stayed, finding a way to love Carter and keep her bond with her family would also be a challenge.

At five on the dot, Phoenix shut down her computer. She was anxious to get to the next morning but had to get through the night first. She looked forward to seeing

Carter after not laying eyes on him all weekend. That was the longest she went without being with him in weeks. Saying good-night to her coworkers, Phoenix bounced out of the building.

Carter was leaning against his car outside her building. The smile that graced her lips radiated from the inside.

"What are you doing here?"

"Ready to start celebrating?"

Phoenix sauntered to him. "Sure."

Carter kissed her passionately right there on the busy city street. "I missed you." He stepped aside and opened the passenger door for her before rounding the front of the car and getting in on the driver's side.

"Where are we going?" she asked.

Carter wouldn't answer. Instead, he laced his fingers in hers as he maneuvered the car into traffic.

Phoenix sat back and enjoyed the ride. Carter filled her in on his busy weekend with the family. She knew their destination was in Manhattan when he crossed the Brooklyn Bridge. Keeping her distracted with conversation, Carter asked her about the call she had with Leah Dresner in the afternoon. She gave him the details about the interview in the morning.

"So I can't keep you up too late tonight?" He winked.

"No. You can't." Phoenix grinned.

Carter rode through busy Manhattan streets, dodging wild-driven yellow cabs as he made his way to Midtown. He pulled into a parking garage on the west side of Sixth Avenue. Carter pulled a duffel bag from the trunk, tossed the keys to the valet, got his ticket and led Phoenix through the garage.

"What's in the bag?" she asked, her curiosity getting the best of her.

"It's for where we're going."

"I figured that. You don't plan on telling me anything, do you?"

"Nope!"

They walked two city blocks to Bryant Park. It looked like hundreds of people were out on the lawn, sitting on blankets. Near the Sixth Avenue side was a massive movie screen.

"Oh, Carter! I've always wanted to do this." She kissed his cheek, not missing a step.

"It's the last one of the season."

They walked around the great lawn in search of the perfect spot. As large as the screen was, any spot would have been fine.

"How about right there?" Phoenix pointed to a spot right near the center.

"This works."

Carter opened the bag and spread the blanket over the grass. Next, he pulled out two glasses, a corkscrew, a prepackaged charcuterie and a bottle of wine. The two of them sat down. They still had time before the movie started.

Carter poured two glasses of wine, handed one to Phoenix, lifted his glass and said, "Cheers."

Phoenix clinked her glass against his.

They sipped and Carter looked deep into her eyes. Phoenix felt as if he were trying to see into her soul.

"You heard me the other night," Carter said matter-of-factly.

"I did," Phoenix admitted.

"I need to know how you feel."

"Honestly. I love you, too, Carter. I never thought I'd say those words ever again."

"They're music to my ears."

"Things are complicated. I'm moving. I've never wanted a long-distance relationship."

"Not if you get this job."

"We both know that's not guaranteed. And what if I do get the job? I'll admit, I want to be with you, but..." Phoenix sighed. "My family. I have yet to hear the end of it after you came to the hospital with me that night. I don't want to feel like I have to choose between you and my own family."

"I'll speak to your family. I owe them that."

"Carter." Phoenix loved him more for saying that but didn't think it would do any good. "I don't know."

"So what, we just keep going on like this? Keeping each other a secret. I want you. All of you. I want to go to family functions with you. Hang out with friends. I want what we had before but better."

"Is that even possible?"

"We won't know if we don't try. The question is, are you willing to try?"

Phoenix looked to the sky. She wanted to try. She wanted to do more than try. Phoenix wanted the same things he wanted. It seemed perfect but reality didn't work that way. "I do, Carter. But—"

"Then let me do my part to fix it."

Phoenix pulled him to her and kissed his lips. She didn't care that they were sitting among hundreds of people in a public New York City park. Carter had done it again. He still had the ability to make her feel like everything would be all right.

Twenty-Eight

Carter paced back and forth in his office at the headquarters as he waited for Phoenix's call. His future with her resided in this job opportunity. When he left that morning, he wished her luck on her interview.

Bill knocked on his open door, catching his attention. "Everything okay, son?"

"Uh. Yeah."

"You're pacing. Is it the business deal?"

"Actually, no."

"Something you want to talk about?"

"You know what? Yes."

Carter closed his office door, gestured for his father to sit and parked himself in his chair. Carter told Bill all about Phoenix.

"The only thing that matters, son, is how you feel for each other. Everyone else will have to get over it. If your heart is leading you back to her, then follow it."

"Thanks, Dad."

"As a man, I agree you need to go to Christopher and Nadine and speak with them. You do owe that to them. Want me to come?"

"No. I'll be fine by myself, but thanks, Dad."

"Anytime." Bill went to stand.

"Dad. Did you come in here for something?"

"Yes." Bill sat back down. "I've been thinking since our talk Sunday. While I'm still disappointed, I'm proud of you. A man has to do what a man has to do. There's nothing like having your own. I wish you the best in your new company and I support you. If you need anything let me know. If it doesn't work out, the door here at Blackwell will always be open for you. Something tells me you won't need to come back. You're a hard worker. You know how to get results. I'm sure you'll do well."

Carter exhaled long and loud. "Thanks, old man. This really means a lot to me."

Bill stood. "Keep me posted on the situation with Phoenix. If you need me, let me know. Most important, take good care of her heart."

"I will."

When Bill left, Carter looked at his watch. Only twenty minutes had passed. Phoenix was still in her interview. Carter needed to get busy, or thinking about Phoenix and this interview would drive him batty.

Carter grabbed his laptop and went to Ethan's office to discuss his conversation with Bill, update him on Phoenix and share some ideas he had about objectives they were looking to meet in this quarter. He'd confided in Ethan and Lincoln about his goals. They'd supported him from the start.

After being with Ethan for a while, Carter's cell phone rang. It was Phoenix.

"How'd it go?"

"You won't believe this. The interview was amazing. They offered me the job and asked me to give them a few days to put together my package. Also, the other job called me back for a second interview. It looks like I'm staying."

"Yes!" Carter pumped his fist. Ethan raised a brow. He forgot he was in his office. "It's time I speak to your family."

Phoenix got quiet. After a while, she said, "Okay. Okay. I'll set it up."

"Before you do?" Carter paused and cleared his throat. "I have to tell you something."

"Lord! Carter, what is it? I don't like the way you said that. You're scaring me." Phoenix huffed.

"It's not like that but I do need to confess something to you."

"Carter!" he could clearly detect the uneasiness in her voice.

"I want to make sure there are never any secrets between us again." He paused again waiting for her to respond.

"I'm listening," Phoenix said.

"I'm the person who made sure Leah Dresner received your information so that you would be considered for the job."

"What? How?"

"Jacob Roberts, the lead investor for my company is also a major investor in the tech start-up that's hiring you. I told them how brilliant you were and he agreed to look at your credentials. That's all I did. You got yourself the job," Carter said.

Phoenix didn't respond for several moments. Carter waited until he couldn't stand the silence anymore.

"I knew you didn't want to move to California and leave your family. I didn't want you to leave me, either. I'll be honest, I wanted to be helpful but I was also self-ish. I may have helped you get the interview, but you're the one who impressed them enough for them to offer you the position so quickly."

Finally Phoenix sighed. Carter was happy to hear some kind of a response even if it wasn't a verbal one.

"I apologize for not saying something before," he con-tinued. "You wouldn't have wanted me to meddle but I don't regret my actions at all. I hope you'll forgive me and I promise that's the last secret I'll ever keep from you."

"Carter…" Phoenix groaned but didn't say anything more.

He wondered what she was going to say. The silence was torture.

"Thank you," she finally said. He could feel her smile through the words.

A broad smile spread across his face. "You're wel-come."

"No more secrets!" she commanded.

"Never again," he agreed.

"See you later," Phoenix said.

"I love you, superwoman." Carter's words lingered for a moment.

"I love you right back."

Together, Carter and Phoenix pulled up in front of her parents' home in Great Neck, Long Island. Phoenix fidgeted the entire ride. And now she looked as if the color had drained from her face. Carter insisted that she invite Savannah and Jaxon, as well.

Carter was nervous but determined. He held Phoenix's hand up the walk. She used her key to enter.

"Mom. Dad."

"In here, honey." They were in the family room. Her mother's tone was clipped. The tension had already begun to rise in the atmosphere.

Phoenix rubbed her hands together and hesitated before walking toward the family room.

"Good evening, Mr. and Mrs. Jones."

"Good evening," Chris said, peering over his glasses. His greeting lacked warmth.

"Mmm-hmm." That was Nadine's greeting. She pursed her lips.

Carter went to Mr. Jones and shook his hand.

"Have a seat, son," Chris said.

Nadine's eyes followed him across the room. Phoenix stayed at the door initially, but then went to sit next to Carter on the sofa.

"What do you want to say to us?" Chris asked.

"Sir, I'd like to start with an apology. Phoenix and I worked things out between us, but I felt it was only right to address this with you directly. I love your daughter. In fact, I've never stopped loving your daughter and I'm not the man I was five years ago. Back then…" Carter told them about Taylor, the baby and why he called off the wedding.

"I can understand that you tried to do what you thought was noble, but there was a better way to handle that. You hurt our daughter, caused us to waste a lot of money and humiliated our family," Chris said.

"I know. I plan to make that up to her."

"M-Mom. Dad."

Nadine peered at Phoenix. "What is it, honey?" Chris said.

"I have something to tell you also."

Nadine's brows furrowed. "Don't tell me you're pregnant!"

"Not now. But I was then."

"What?" Chris and Nadine said at the same time. Nadine scooted to the edge of her seat.

"What are you talking about?"

"I was pregnant. I wanted to surprise Carter on our wedding night, but the wedding never happened. I was so hurt and angry. I wouldn't let him explain why he was calling off the wedding." Both Nadine and Chris's mouths hung open. Each leaned in, taking in every word that fell from Phoenix's mouth. She swallowed. "I should have said something that night but I didn't. I just needed to think. I figured going to Belize by myself would give me a chance to get my thoughts together. But when I got back I had the miscarriage…"

Just then, Savannah and Jaxon walked into the room.

"Did you know about this?" Nadine asked Savannah.

Savannah nodded.

Phoenix continued. "I didn't know what else to do. The doctor said there could have been several reasons for the miscarriage, including stress. I should have said something." Tears fell from Phoenix's eyes. Carter took one hand in his and used his free hand to rub comforting circles on her back. "He thought he was doing the right thing by being a father. I understand that. Unfortunately, that baby turned out not to be his, and I lost our baby. Had I heard him out that night, maybe this could have been avoided. Who knows?"

"Mr. and Mrs. Jones, Phoenix and I have a second

chance here and we want to take it. I promise all of you that I will handle her heart with care."

"Phoenix." Chris looked intently at his daughter. "Is this what you want?"

"Yes, Dad. It is." She looked from her father to Carter. At that moment Carter felt all the love he held for her.

"Phoenix, are you sure?"

"I am, Mom."

"Well, you two are going to have to work on your communication skills." Chris chuckled and the weight enveloping the room lifted.

"Chris, what will people think?" Nadine said with a hand on her heart.

"Honey, it doesn't matter what people think. What matters is that they love each other. My concern is her happiness. If he makes her happy, then so be it." Chris looked at Carter. "And that this young man is responsible for our daughter's heart." He pointed at Carter. "Don't you forget that. I'll be watching."

"Never," Carter said. "I will never forget that or the responsibility that comes with that. With your blessing—" Carter pulled a box from his suit jacket "—I want to ask Phoenix again, if she would do me the honor of being my wife."

Phoenix's mouth fell open. She covered it with both hands. "Oh my goodness, Carter!"

"That would be up to my daughter. Right, Phoenix?" Chris said.

"It would," Nadine cosigned.

Phoenix looked at everyone in the room. A slick smile slid across Savannah's face. "You knew about this?" Phoenix asked.

"Of course." Savannah snickered. Phoenix narrowed her eyes at her sister.

Phoenix turned to Carter. “That’s why you insisted she come.” Phoenix teasingly rolled her eyes at Savannah.

Unfazed, Savannah laughed. “Answer the man.”

“Phoenix, will you marry me?”

“Yes! Yes. I will marry you!” Phoenix wrapped her arms around Carter’s neck and squeezed him tight. He couldn’t wait to get his fiancée home.

* * * * *

WE HOPE YOU ENJOYED THIS BOOK FROM

HARLEQUIN DESIRE

Luxury, scandal, desire—welcome to the lives of the American elite.

Be transported to the worlds of oil barons, family dynasties, moguls and celebrities. Get ready for juicy plot twists, delicious sensuality and intriguing scandal.

6 NEW BOOKS AVAILABLE EVERY MONTH!

HDHALO2021

Uplifting or passionate, heartfelt or thrilling— Harlequin has your happily-ever-after.

With a wide range of romance series that each offer new books every month, you are sure to find the satisfying escape you deserve.

Look for all Harlequin series new releases on the *last Tuesday* of each month in stores and online!

Harlequin.com

HONSALE0521

COMING NEXT MONTH FROM

HARLEQUIN

DESIRE

#2821 HOW TO CATCH A BAD BOY

Texas Cattleman's Club: Heir Apparent • by Cat Schield

Private Investigator Lani Li must get up close and personal with her onetime lover, former playboy Asher Edmond, who's accused of embezzling—and insists he's innocent. With suspicions—and chemistry—building, can she get the job done without losing her heart a second time?

#2822 SECRETS OF A ONE NIGHT STAND

Billionaires of Boston • by Naima Simone

After one hot night with a handsome stranger, business executive Mycah Hill doesn't expect to see him again. Then she starts her new job and he's her *boss*, CEO Achilles Farrell. But keeping things professional is hard when she learns she's having his child...

#2823 BLIND DATE WITH THE SPARE HEIR

Locketts of Tuxedo Park • by Yahrah St. John

Elyse Robinson believes the powerful Lockett family swindled her father. And when her blind date is second son Dr. Julian Lockett, it's her chance to find the family's weaknesses—but it turns out Julian is *her* weakness. With sparks flying, will she choose love or loyalty?

#2824 THE FAKE ENGAGEMENT FAVOR

The Texas Tremaines • by Charlene Sands

When country music superstar Gage Tremaine's reputation is rocked by scandal, he needs a fake fiancée fast to win back fans. Family friend and former nemesis college professor Gianna Marino is perfect for the role—until their very real chemistry becomes impossible to ignore...

#2825 WAYS TO TEMPT THE BOSS

Brooklyn Nights • by Joanne Rock

CEO Lucas Deschamps needs to protect his family's cosmetics business by weeding out a corporate spy, and he suspects new employee Blair Wescott. He's determined to find the truth by getting closer to her—but the heat between them may be a temptation he can't resist...

#2826 BEST LAID WEDDING PLANS

Moonlight Ridge • by Karen Booth

Resort wedding planner Autumn Kincaid is a hopeless romantic even after being left at the altar. Grey Holloway is Mr. Grump and a new partner in the resort. Now that he's keeping an eye on her, sparks ignite, but will their differences derail everything?

YOU CAN FIND MORE INFORMATION ON UPCOMING HARLEQUIN TITLES, FREE EXCERPTS AND MORE AT HARLEQUIN.COM.

HDCNM0821

SPECIAL EXCERPT FROM

HARLEQUIN

DESIRE

After one hot night with a handsome stranger, business executive Mycah Hill doesn't expect to see him again. Then she starts her new job and he's her boss, CEO Achilles Farrell. But keeping things professional is hard when she learns she's having his child...

Read on for a sneak peek at
Secrets of a One Night Stand
by USA TODAY *bestselling author Naima Simone.*

"You're staring again."

"I am." Mycah switched her legs, recrossing them. And damn his too-observant gaze, he didn't miss the gesture. Probably knew why she did it, too. Not that the action alleviated the sweet pain pulsing inside her. "Does it still bother you?"

"Depends."

"On?"

"Why you're staring."

She slicked the tip of her tongue over her lips, an unfamiliar case of nerves making themselves known. Again, his eyes caught the tell, dropping to her mouth, resting there, and the blast of heat that exploded inside her damn near fused her to the bar stool. What he did with one look… Jesus, it wasn't fair. Not to her. Not to humankind.

"Because you're so stareable. Don't do that," she insisted, no, *implored* when he stiffened, his eyes going glacial. Frustration stormed inside her, swirling and releasing in a sharp clap of laughter. She huffed out a breath, shaking her head. "You should grant me leeway because you don't know me, and I don't know you. And you, all of you—" she waved her hand up and down, encompassing his long, below-the-shoulder-length hair, his massive shoulders, his thick thighs and his large booted feet "—are a lot."

"A lot of what?" His body didn't loosen, his face remaining shuttered. But that voice…

She shivered. It had deepened to a growl, and her breath caught.

"A lot of—" she spread out her arms the length of his shoulders "—mass. A lot of attitude." She exhaled, her hands dropping to her thighs. "A lot of beauty," she murmured, and it contained a slight tremble she hated but couldn't erase. "A lot of pride. A lot of..." Fire. Darkness. Danger. Shelter.

Her fingers curled into her palm.

"A lot of intensity," she finished. Lamely. Jesus, so lamely.

Achilles stared at her. And she fought not to fidget under his hooded gaze. Struggled to remain still as he leaned forward and that tantalizing, woodsy scent beckoned her closer seconds before he did.

"Mycah, come here."

She should be rebelling; she should be stiffening in offense at that rumbled order. Should be. But no. Instead, a weight she hadn't consciously been aware of tumbled off her shoulders. Allowing her to breathe deeper...freer. Because as Achilles gripped the lapel of her jacket and drew her closer, wrinkling the silk, he also slowly peeled away Mycah Hill, the business executive who helmed and carried the responsibilities of several departments... Mycah Hill, the eldest daughter of Laurence and Cherise Hill, who bore the burden of their financial irresponsibility and unrealistic expectations.

In their place stood Mycah, the vulnerable stripped-bare woman who wanted to let go. Who *could* let go. Just this once.

So as he reeled her in, she went, willingly, until their faces hovered barely an inch apart. Until their breaths mingled. Until his bright gaze heated her skin.

This close, she glimpsed the faint smattering of freckles across the tops of his lean cheeks and the high bridge of his nose. The light cinnamon spots should've detracted from the sensual brutality of his features. But they didn't. In an odd way, they enhanced it.

Had her wanting to dot each one with the top of her tongue.

"What?" she whispered.

"Say it again." He released her jacket and trailed surprisingly gentle fingers up her throat. "I want to find out for myself what the lie tastes like on your mouth."

Lust flashed inside her, hot, searing. Consuming.

God, she liked it. This...*consuming*.

If she wasn't careful, she could easily come to crave it.

Don't miss what happens next in...
Secrets of a One Night Stand *by Naima Simone, the next book in the Billionaires of Boston series!*

Available September 2021 wherever Harlequin Desire books and ebooks are sold.

Harlequin.com

Copyright © 2021 by Naima Simone

HDEXP0821

Get 4 FREE REWARDS!

We'll send you 2 FREE Books <u>plus</u> 2 FREE Mystery Gifts.

Harlequin Desire books transport you to the world of the American elite with juicy plot twists, delicious sensuality and intriguing scandal.

YES! Please send me 2 FREE Harlequin Desire novels and my 2 FREE gifts (gifts are worth about $10 retail). After receiving them, if I don't wish to receive any more books, I can return the shipping statement marked "cancel." If I don't cancel, I will receive 6 brand-new novels every month and be billed just $4.55 per book in the U.S. or $5.24 per book in Canada. That's a savings of at least 13% off the cover price! It's quite a bargain! Shipping and handling is just 50¢ per book in the U.S. and $1.25 per book in Canada.* I understand that accepting the 2 free books and gifts places me under no obligation to buy anything. I can always return a shipment and cancel at any time. The free books and gifts are mine to keep no matter what I decide.

225/326 HDN GNND

Name (please print)

Address Apt. #

City State/Province Zip/Postal Code

Email: Please check this box ☐ if you would like to receive newsletters and promotional emails from Harlequin Enterprises ULC and its affiliates. You can unsubscribe anytime.

Mail to the **Harlequin Reader Service:**
IN U.S.A.: P.O. Box 1341, Buffalo, NY 14240-8531
IN CANADA: P.O. Box 603, Fort Erie, Ontario L2A 5X3

Want to try 2 free books from another series? Call 1-800-873-8635 or visit www.ReaderService.com.

*Terms and prices subject to change without notice. Prices do not include sales taxes, which will be charged (if applicable) based on your state or country of residence. Canadian residents will be charged applicable taxes. Offer not valid in Quebec. This offer is limited to one order per household. Books received may not be as shown. Not valid for current subscribers to Harlequin Desire books. All orders subject to approval. Credit or debit balances in a customer's account(s) may be offset by any other outstanding balance owed by or to the customer. Please allow 4 to 6 weeks for delivery. Offer available while quantities last.

Your Privacy—Your information is being collected by Harlequin Enterprises ULC, operating as Harlequin Reader Service. For a complete summary of the information we collect, how we use this information and to whom it is disclosed, please visit our privacy notice located at corporate.harlequin.com/privacy-notice. From time to time we may also exchange your personal information with reputable third parties. If you wish to opt out of this sharing of your personal information, please visit readerservice.com/consumerschoice or call 1-800-873-8635. **Notice to California Residents**—Under California law, you have specific rights to control and access your data. For more information on these rights and how to exercise them, visit corporate.harlequin.com/california-privacy.

HD21R

IF YOU ENJOYED THIS BOOK
WE THINK YOU WILL ALSO LOVE

HARLEQUIN
PRESENTS

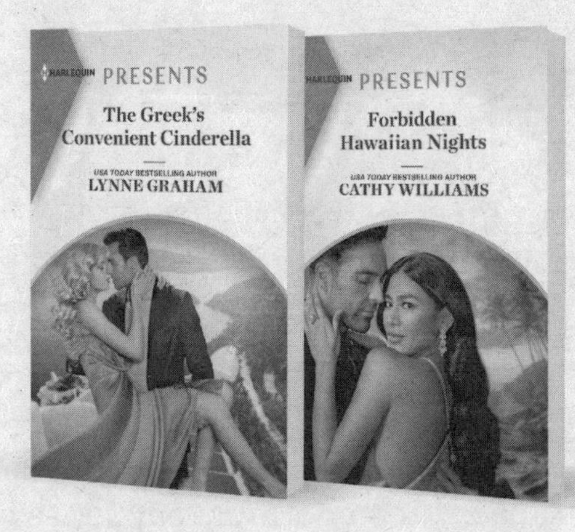

Escape to exotic locations where passion knows no bounds.

Welcome to the glamorous lives of royals and billionaires, where passion knows no bounds. Be swept into a world of luxury, wealth and exotic locations.

8 NEW BOOKS AVAILABLE EVERY MONTH!

HPXSERIES2021

Love Harlequin romance?

DISCOVER.

Be the first to find out about promotions, news and exclusive content!

ReaderService.com

EXPLORE.

Sign up for the Harlequin e-newsletter and download a free book from any series at **TryHarlequin.com**

CONNECT.

Join our Harlequin community to share your thoughts and connect with other romance readers!
Facebook.com/groups/HarlequinConnection

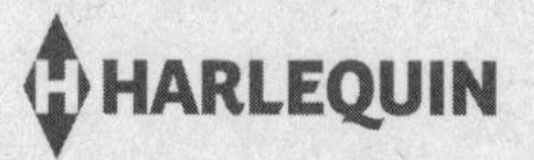

HSOCIAL2021